HOLD ME CLOSE

A CHARMED BRACELET TALE

LARA ARCHER

SAGITTA PRESS

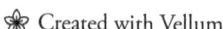

CHAPTER 1

$\mathcal{A}$pparently, a woman could drape herself in silk from shoulders to ankles, and still feel stark naked.

After eighteen months in mourning, color seemed obscene, even the soft shade of blue Julia had chosen. She longed for the numb, comforting cover of her widow's blacks, but just that morning Christopher's Aunt Margaret had told her, kindly but firmly, "You must give them up now, Julia, dear. I begin to feel we've a storm cloud hovering permanently in the parlor."

So here Julia was, dressed for dancing in a ballroom hung with hothouse garlands, the chandeliers dazzling bright, and a parade of men seizing her by the waist to wheel her across the floor.

Twenty-six was far too young to shut herself up forever— of *course* it was—but still her heart ached as all the strange male hands pressing her spine only served to remind her that Christopher would never hold her in his arms again.

"Come now, darling," said Aunt Margaret, when yet another gentleman returned Julia to the chairs at the side of the room. "What's the use of wearing colors if you look so glum? You'd be the loveliest lady here, if only you'd smile and laugh as you used to."

Used to.

Yes, that was the operative phrase. *I used to be so happy. I used to believe my life was charmed. I used to have the love of my life beside me each day.*

Aunt Margaret took both of Julia's hands in her own and squeezed gently. "Oh, my sweet girl. Christopher loved you, with all his heart," she said. "I never saw him so happy as the day he married you. But it would break his heart now to see you wither away like this."

Julia blinked. "Is that what you think I'm doing? Withering away?"

Aunt Margaret merely sighed.

Oh, dear. Had she been as bad as all that?

No, Christopher would not approve in the slightest. But if she was withering, she had no idea how to stop. Not without him.

Aunt Margaret glanced up suddenly, spotting something over Julia's shoulder, in the direction of the ballroom staircase. "Good gracious!" she cried. "How on earth can *he* be here?"

Julia swiveled in her seat, her foolish heart leaping with the same ridiculous hope that seized her from time to time—that somehow, miraculously, Christopher was walking into the room, healthy and whole, his kind blue eyes sparkling with life.

But of course it wasn't Christopher who'd entered.

That crushing certainty descended as it always did—this time followed by an equally unpleasant sensation as she recognized the man who *had*.

Major Holsworth.

Looking fierce as ever with his jet-black hair and jet-black eyes, Holsworth stood half a head taller than the next tallest man present, and at least a hand span broader. He glared down at the crowd with a hard look that belonged to a battlefield, not a ballroom, as though he were deciding where to aim the next fusillade of cannon fire.

Julia's pulse thudded dully, with something like fear. It had always been a mystery to her how that man and Christopher could have been such devoted friends, as close as brothers, almost all their lives.

"You did not *invite* him, did you, Aunt?" she whispered under her breath. "Without telling me?"

"Of course not," said Aunt Margaret in a jubilant voice, tugging Julia by the elbow to follow her towards the stairs. "I thought the dear boy was still in India."

"Dear Boy" was the last description Julia would have applied to the glowering giant stalking down the steps. "Savage Beast" would fit him better. Or perhaps "Black Pirate." Yes, it would be quite easy to imagine Holsworth in a red silk waistcoat with a cutlass clamped between his teeth. Every instinct bid Julia to make like a merchant ship and steer clear of his path.

But Aunt Margaret could not be gainsaid, and in a few moments more, Julia found herself making her curtsy to the man who'd always sent a chill down her spine. He bowed over her hand and then leaned down to kiss Aunt Margaret on the cheek. Dear Lord—Holsworth had acquired quite a scar on the left side of his face since last they'd met, starting at the outside corner of his eye and slanting over his cheekbone. He looked more fearsome and piratical than ever.

Aunt Margaret, though, beamed at him as if he were a visiting archangel. "Oh, Marcus," she exclaimed. "I cannot say how wonderful it is to see you, whole and safe and home in Devonshire! You are a hero, so all the London papers say!"

An odd expression flickered across Major Holsworth's harsh features. "I suppose that is what they call it, Lady

Lambert," he said, in that deep, gruff voice of his, the voice that always seemed to rumble strangely through Julia's belly.

"It most certainly *is* what they call it," Aunt Margaret insisted. "And I expect you shall be granted a knighthood as well. You and your men ensured a victory for civilization."

"A victory for superior artillery, madam," said Major Holsworth, his tone almost grudging. "In any case, the British authorities in India shall not be troubled by Pindari fighters again."

Aunt Margaret nodded. "Christopher would have rejoiced to know the government is secure at long last. An India unified and at peace was his life's work and constant dream."

Holsworth drew a ragged breath at the mention of his old friend's name, and his dark eyes gleamed. "I must offer my condolences for the loss of your nephew, Lady Lambert. Christopher Grantleigh was the very best of men."

"The loss is yours as much as mine, dear boy," Aunt Margaret responded, laying a palm to the major's tanned cheek, apparently untroubled by his scar. "And you owe me no more condolences—your letters were the greatest comfort to me in those first dark weeks."

Letters? Aunt Margaret hadn't shared any such letters with her, but Julia supposed it wasn't entirely surprising Holsworth had written them. Christopher often told her how Holsworth had come to live at Grantleigh Hall when both of them were eight years old, after their fathers perished together trying to rescue horses from a stable fire. Margaret —widowed young herself and returned to her childhood home—joined forces with her maiden sister Eleanor to serve as second mothers to the boys. When the time came, the two women provided funds to send Holsworth to Cambridge alongside the young earl. Aunt Eleanor's devotion even inspired her to take up residence in Calcutta once Holsworth made his life there.

As far as Christopher had been concerned, he and Holsworth were truly brothers—though men more different than aristocratic, golden-haired Christopher and this rough-looking son of a freehold farmer would be difficult to imagine.

"Holsworth can be intimidating," Christopher had warned her just after their engagement, when Major Holsworth was about to make one of his rare visits home to England. "But I know he will love you, Julia, truly, just as I do."

In truth, the six weeks of Holsworth's leave made her feel she was trapped in a pen with an ill-tempered bull. Holsworth's gaze was so fierce, his huge body tensed with a tight, leashed energy, as if he might charge at the least provocation and trample her. She'd catch him looking at her from time to time, always with a grim expression, and she couldn't help thinking that he disapproved mightily of his friend's choice of bride.

Nonetheless, for her future husband's sake, she'd tried to charm the man. Christopher swore Holsworth possessed both a keen intelligence and an excellent sense of humor, so she offered her wittiest conversation, but her best efforts to sparkle were met with rather pained looks, at most a tight smile. Though once, just once, when she'd made an offhand quip about how Lord Darby always surveilled his guests as though he expected someone to pilfer the candlesticks, Holsworth's eyes lit for an instant, and a genuine laugh escaped him, giving her a glimpse of what Christopher must love in his friend. But it was like watching a scrap of paper catch fire—a momentary flare, quickly turned black and stiff and cold again. In fact, Holsworth cut short his visit and returned to his regiment the next day.

Then two years ago in London, the last time the three of them met, Holsworth and Christopher had quarreled quite fiercely. After dinner, Christopher sent Julia off to bed on her own, which had never been their habit. She couldn't fall asleep without him, and that was why she overheard the men's raised voices downstairs in Christopher's study. Their words were impossible to make out, but the angry tone was unmistakable. After a while, Major Holsworth's heavy boot-heels slammed their way across the marble foyer floor, and then his voice rose up to her ears quite clearly, dark and furious: "I warn you, Chris! You will live to regret this!"

Christopher never said a word to her afterwards about this falling out. Holsworth returned once more to his post in Calcutta, and Christopher returned to his work in the House of Lords, and Julia was quite relieved not to have to think about the matter again.

Remembering Holsworth's words now, though, they seemed more sinister than they had at the time. Barely six months after they were spoken, Christopher was dead.

But, no, any suspicious feeling on her part was ridiculous. Christopher's doctors said his unrelenting work schedule had stressed a heart already weakened by childhood rheumatic fever, and brought on the inflammation that claimed his life. And besides, Holsworth was far off in the mountains of India at the time. Little as she liked the man, his argument with her husband that night was an unhappy coincidence, nothing more.

In the ballroom now, Holsworth turned to Julia and his dark eyes met hers directly, sending an uncomfortable jolt through her. His gaze flicked lower, taking in the length of her body, and her flesh tingled as though the silk of her gown had turned entirely transparent.

Blast him. He had no business unsettling her so.

"You've grown too thin, Lady Grantleigh," Holsworth said gravely, his expression almost accusing.

Blast him twice. The state of her figure was no business of his. Despite his spotless scarlet-and-gold uniform and his perfect soldier's posture, he clearly had things to learn about genteel ballroom behavior.

Aunt Margaret sighed again. "I can scarce get the girl to eat," she said, her own manners apparently forgotten in Holsworth's presence. Then her eyes suddenly sparkled, and she gestured toward the pairs of dancers moving to the center of the room as the orchestra paused to re-tune their instruments. "But, look! The waltz is about to start! Please, Marcus, do an old woman's heart some good and let me see you dance with darling Julia. She needs something to lift her spirits."

Major Holsworth's brows shot up in apparent alarm, and Julia felt just as taken aback. The last thing to lift her spirits would be Holsworth's huge body in such close proximity to her own. To her own *too thin* one, apparently.

Before the man could form a polite response, Julia hurried to say, "No, please, Aunt. This talk of Christopher has been distressing for me. I need a few moments to myself, if you don't mind."

Aunt Margaret frowned. "Oh, *Julia.*"

"I promise, I will return in a few minutes," she said. Surely the waltzes would be over if she could delay just half an hour. "And perhaps then...a quadrille or a Scotch reel? If Major Holsworth is amenable." Anything that limited their contact to a few touches of the hands would be vastly preferable to the waltz.

Holsworth managed a surprisingly courtly bow. "It shall be as the whim of the musicians dictates, Lady Grantleigh." And now his mouth quirked with a touch of wry irony, causing that cruel scar on his cheek to bend like a drawn bow.

Julia's belly twanged at the sight of it.

She curtsied again and hurried off, hoping it wasn't too obvious she was fleeing.

After the overheated ballroom, the hallways and the staircase felt cold, especially since she was dressed so lightly. Her skin pebbled to gooseflesh. But a chill was well worth it if she could escape into privacy again. The public evening had taken even more of a toll on her than she'd expected.

She bolted up the stairs like a rabbit with a fox on its heels, and shoved her bedroom door closed behind her as though to fend off teeth and claws. The moment she was alone, a well of emotion rushed up from the pit of her stomach, the sort that had so often made her burst out in sobs during the first year of her widowhood.

Before the tears could come, though, a startling sight distracted her: the fireplace was in full blaze.

And the lamp by her bed was lit.

Odd. She'd snuffed the lamp herself just before she went downstairs for the dancing, and she'd watched the chambermaid bank the embers in the hearth. The room should have been dark and cool, but instead it was warm and full of light.

Someone entered my chamber while I was downstairs.

She scanned the room quickly, but she was quite alone.

And yet she felt …*something*, a sort of presence. A sort of weight in the air. Not threatening, she realized as she let the feeling settle over her, but *comforting* somehow. Like a soft shawl draped over her shoulders.

Protective. Warm and safe.

"Christopher?" she whispered.

Even as she spoke his name, she felt foolish. Of course the sensation she felt was just the relief of returning to her sanctuary, and the fire's unexpected warmth on her chilled skin. No doubt Aunt Margaret had anticipated her early retreat to her chamber, and had instructed a footman to come and light the lamp and build the fire high again.

Nonetheless, the sensation of solace was too sweet to dismiss. Indulging herself just a few moments more, she stepped towards the fireplace, holding her palms up to feel the waves of heat.

And that was when she saw it.

A little box.

A little carved wooden box, a few inches square, sitting on the tiles of the hearth, gleaming in the firelight.

Scarcely able to breathe, she stepped closer still to look at it more carefully.

A thousand thoughts scrambled through her head at once. Christopher had collected carved objects like this, sent to England from India, where he always dreamed of going himself, if only his uncertain health had allowed it. He'd given her many such gifts over the years: a beautiful rosewood mirror and hairbrush, a mahogany frame for a miniature of their wedding portrait, small carved bowls in which she kept her rings and earbobs, the teak letter tray inlaid with starbursts made of brass. Those sweet little gifts were her most beloved treasures, far more precious to her than the fabled Grantleigh Sapphires or the heaps of other jewels he'd given her.

Her heart thumped hard, and her head felt light.

Half afraid it would vanish if she touched it, she bent over and picked the box up.

It was solid in her hand—unquestionably real. And the carving was magnificent once she could see it up close: the edges of the lid lined with dozens of perfect little lotus blossoms, and in the center, in delicate relief, the figure of a woman.

And, *goodness*, what a woman. The figure was caught in the motion of a dance, and wore no clothing beyond a pair of flowing pantaloons that scarcely covered her hips and thighs. Her arms curved outwards, one ankle crossed over the other knee, and one rounded hip was thrust to the side. Tiny beads of inlaid ivory formed a cascading necklace over her bare breasts and belly, and she wore a crown and girdle of inlaid filigreed gold, with gold bracelets about her wrists.

Sensual and serene all at once.

A warm blush crept up Julia's throat. Her husband had never given her an object decorated quite like this one. She'd only ever seen such voluptuous figures painted in some of the fine old Indian manuscripts Christopher kept in his private library, which she'd dared look at just the one time when she was packing away his things.

Oh, but the box was beautiful, and very old, with a rich patina that nothing but time could bring. She brushed her fingers over the satiny surface, breathed in the subtle scent —*sandalwood*.

So lovely.

But where on earth had it come from?

Much as her heart longed to believe Christopher had somehow sent her one last gift, her reason sought a more earthly explanation.

The box had come from India, that was clear enough.

And who had just arrived from India?

Her stomach twisted, and she almost threw the thing into the fire.

Holsworth.

But why would Holsworth give this to her? From her husband, the gift, with its erotic carving, would have been uncharacteristically risqué, but romantic. From a man to whom she wasn't married, it would be…*shocking*. Beyond shocking. Were Christopher still alive, he'd call the offender out with pistols at dawn.

Even Major Holsworth, rough as he was, would know that.

Julia fought to calm her jangling nerves. It was nearly unimaginable that Holsworth would do something so scandalous as to come into her private chamber and leave this box.

And yet—she glanced again at the blazing fire, at her lamp glowing bright beside her bed, and a new suspicion prickled. Good Lord, Holsworth hadn't done that, too, had he? He hadn't meant to *join* her here, for some sort of secret assignation?

She whirled to face the door.

But it was still closed tight, and the hall outside was silent.

Oh, for pity's sake—of course he hadn't intended anything of the sort. He'd never shown the least interest in her that way. And falling out or no falling out, he had always been Christopher's *best friend.* Surely a man with the least shred of honor would not shame his friend's widow so egregiously.

In any case, he could scarcely have come up here undetected—when he arrived at Grantleigh Hall, a footman would have ushered him directly to the ballroom. And even if he evaded the servants, how could he guess which bedroom in this great old house was currently hers? Months ago, she'd moved from the rooms meant for the lord and lady of the house, in preparation for the day when young Alfred, Christopher's cousin and heir, finished at Cambridge and came to claim his seat.

Her suspicions were perfectly ridiculous.

And yet, a potent image filled her mind, of Holsworth sweeping through the door, huge and hulking, stalking towards her, seizing her by the waist with his powerful arms, and opening his mouth over hers.

Her head spun, and a strange pulse went through her belly.

No, no—her emotions were overwrought tonight, that was all. Holsworth had come to Grantleigh Hall to offer condolences, not to seduce her. Any moment now, a perfectly rational explanation for the appearance of the box was going to present itself to her mind, and everything would feel normal again.

She glanced back at the wooden object in her palm, at the inlaid gold glimmering and sparking in the glow of the fire.

Of course—the box itself might contain the answer to her questions. She set her hand to the lid and pulled it loose.

And gasped.

Inside, nested in a swirl of red velvet, lay a gold bracelet.

It was an unusually warm, bright shade of gold, gleaming in the firelight. It was as intricately carved as the box that held it, and presumably as old.

Gingerly, she lifted the bracelet out, and held it up before the flames. Despite its apparent age, it was flawless, without a scratch or bit of tarnish.

Unlike the thin, fragile Indian bangles Christopher had given her in the past, this was a broad, graceful oval, and rather heavy—its surface half an inch wide, engraved with a swirling pattern of leaves and flowers.

It must have been made for an extremely small-boned woman, though. Julia was quite slim, as Holsworth had so rudely reminded her this evening, but the oval opening still looked too narrow to pass over her hand.

She spun it round to see the other side, and found an elaborate, curving script carved into that surface. *Sanskrit.* Familiar from Christopher's Indian library, though she herself had never learned to read the language.

She frowned. The bracelet was as much a puzzle as the box.

And yet, her hand fairly itched to slip the golden oval on.

A silly impulse—she couldn't possibly keep it without knowing exactly who had left it here. And, in any case, it was much too small. Even with her fingers bunched, she couldn't slide it past her second row of knuckles.

Her eye followed the curve of metal round and round, mesmerized by its beauty. And that was when she noticed little seams at either end of the oval, hidden within the swirls of the leaves. And—*ah*—a tiny gold pin beside one of the seams, protruding just above the smooth surface.

A push on the pin with the edge of her fingernail, and, *yes*, the seams popped open—one of them concealing a tiny hinge, the other a heavy, curved gold wire along which the two hollow halves of the bracelet could slide apart. A clever mechanism. It let her widen the oval just enough to slide her whole hand through.

She pressed the two halves together again, and they joined with a click, the seams vanishing neatly into the swirl of leaves again.

Now the bracelet fit her wrist as though it were made for her. Not tight—it hung just slightly loose over her wrist bone, enough to slide an inch or two down towards her elbow—but not wide enough either to pass back over the heel of her hand.

And, oh, it really was lovely.

The shining glow of it beside the fire was the very color of—of *happiness*, yes, embodied happiness. A giddy thought, but accurate, somehow. And the metal must have absorbed the heat from the hearth, because it was warm as sunlight against her skin.

An ache filled her heart to think of Christopher and his gifts.

But, oddly enough, it wasn't the sad sort of ache she was used to.

This was a different sort of *pleasant* ache. A kind of yearning hopefulness. A note of joy she hadn't felt in a very, very long time.

How strange.

And how wonderful.

It made no sense at all, but suddenly, she felt an urge to go back downstairs to the dancing, to the room full of voices and music and laughter. To be human and alive again.

She didn't let herself stop to think. She knew the impulse would vanish quick as a mist if she didn't go right now. Aunt Margaret had spoken truly—Christopher would have hated to see her wither away. After a year and a half of deep mourning, he would have wanted her to feel joy again.

She was like a seedling in a drought, and a sudden shower of rain was falling. She needed to let it in.

Decency demanded that she take off the bracelet before appearing in public again, since she did not know the identity of the giver, but she didn't stop to do that either. She felt just a little wicked, though she did at least tuck the sandalwood box into her private jewelry cabinet where the half-naked dancer couldn't scandalize her maids. Gathering her skirts in her hand, she dashed back down the stairs to the foyer, and hurried towards the west wing staircase that led down into the ballroom.

The route took her along the darkened windows of the conservatory, and as she passed, the arm on which she wore the bracelet happened to bump one of the panes of glass. The bracelet chimed brightly against the pane, and suddenly a new impulse seized her: she would go through the conservatory to the private stairs at the back, and enter the ballroom more secretly that way. It felt more adventurous somehow, and she needed a bit of adventure.

She slipped through the door to the gallery where rows of palms and orange trees made exotic, scented shadows in the moonlight. The air, sultry thanks to the brass pipes along the walls circulating heated water, felt lovely and summer-like against her bare arms. She'd walked here so often in the sunlit hours of the day, she could find her way easily enough, and scarcely slowed her steps.

Which was why, when she saw a huge, dark, terrifying form suddenly emerge in her path, she had no chance to stop herself from running straight into it.

CHAPTER 2

*B*efore Julia had time to scream, a great weight struck her, and she was knocked to the ground. Rough hands were at her throat, and a low, harsh voice demanded, "Who are you, and what are you doing here?"

He might not have recognized her, but she knew instantly who her assailant was.

"*Holsworth!*" she hissed with what little breath she was able to draw, even while instinct had her twisting to free her arms and legs from the warm bulk pinning her to the floor. Her backside and shoulders throbbed from where they'd hit the hard marble. "You will get off me this instant!"

The huge dark form above her stiffened, and the hands that had been about to throttle her flew back. "Good God!" Holsworth's deep voice swore. "Julia—Lady *Grantleigh!*" And she could feel the desperate tension in his body as he sought to scramble away.

It was a relief to be released from the crush of his weight, but as he tried to rise, her left wrist was tugged awkwardly along with him.

"Wait!" she cried. "My—my bracelet is caught. Don't pull!"

He froze in place, still hovering just inches over her, his palms now pressed to the floor on either side of her shoulders, his knees on either side of her thighs, covering her, but somehow managing to avoid actually touching her again. "*What*?"

"My bracelet!" A hot blush burned from her very core. The thoughts she'd had about him entering her chamber upstairs made her want to shrink away in shame. "It's—oh, I think my bracelet's snagged somehow. On your—your uniform coat."

In fact, his coat was the least of her worries. Judging from the warm air against her calves, the hem of her gown was jumbled all the way up around her knees. And Holsworth was so close she could catch the scent of his cologne, a warm mix of bay leaf and leather, with a hint of some tropical spice. The intimacy of their position was…*simply too much*. Somehow worse in the darkness than it would have been in the light.

Holsworth shifted his weight carefully onto one knee, and took her wrist in one of his big hands. She could feel his fingers working their way around the bracelet, seeking the spot where it had attached itself to his uniform.

If only there were enough light for her to see his face. If he were the one who'd put the mysterious bracelet in her chambers, he'd surely recognize it by touch, and she wanted to see his expression when he realized what it was.

Using her free hand to push up slightly off the floor, she managed to wriggle her way to something more approaching a seated posture, and to her relief, Holsworth squatted back on his haunches to give her room. Her forearm was still pinned to his chest, of course. And her legs were still trapped between his, with no easy way to extricate them without knocking the man over, at least until the bracelet was released and she had the use of both her arms again.

Good heavens, he was a *big* man, especially at such close quarters as this. Christopher had been only a little taller than she was, and lean of frame. The size and power of Holsworth's body was a different thing entirely—he seemed to *loom*, to *threaten*, whether he wished to or not, the sheer mass and heat of him dominating all the available space.

Blast it. Much as she wanted to know whether he'd given her the mysterious gift, her nerves longed for him to get the bracelet loose so she'd be free of him as well.

His fingers made another circuit of the gold oval, his touch hot whenever it brushed her wrist. "I don't understand how it's managed to catch on me at all," he said at last. "The surface feels smooth all the way around."

"It—it has hidden closures," she said. Surely that information would identify the bracelet for him, if he was in fact the source of it. Her heart beat a little harder than before. "There's a concealed hinge at one end, and a pin at the other that lets the two halves slide apart. Some part of that mechanism must be stuck in the fabric of your coat."

"One side seems stuck in the cloth of my shirt as well," he growled, giving the bracelet an experimental tug. "It won't give way on either end. Good Lord, you women find the most infernally complicated ways of ornamenting yourselves."

Well, *that* answered her question: the tone of simple masculine irritation made it quite clear the bracelet hadn't come from him.

"I can't get it loose," he said, tugging again. "And we certainly cannot stay here on this floor." Without waiting for a reply, he let go of the bracelet and seized her waist with both hands. Then he simply *stood*, his powerful arms sweeping her to her feet as easily as if she were a china doll.

Her stomach lurched and her lungs seemed to bump her ribs, and worst of all, standing didn't render their posture appreciably more appropriate. With her bracelet still snagged, they stood close as lovers, his arms about her, her forearm pressed to his chest with her fingers all but brushing the underside of his jaw.

And, Lord, much as she really, truly did want to get away from him, some deeper, less civilized part of her was having other impulses entirely. Holsworth was so warm and strong and solid, so utterly male, she felt the strangest urge to bury her face against his chest and breathe in more of his cologne.

Which she *most certainly* would not allow herself to do.

At least gravity had dropped her skirts more or less into the correct position again.

Still, she really did need to dispel the enforced intimacy of the moment. "Generally speaking," she said, in the arch tone she might use at a formal dinner, "it's *men* who make the ornaments ladies wear. Ladies are in fact *obliged* to wear them, to shore up masculine pride."

"Is that so?" he answered, this time giving the bracelet and his lapel a simultaneous, and still quite ineffectual, pull. "And who obliged you to wear this particular one? And why now, precisely? You weren't wearing a bracelet earlier tonight."

She raised her brows, though she doubted he could see them in the darkness. "You made an inventory of the jewelry I was wearing?"

A pause. "Not of your jewelry specifically," he said. "But soldiers learn to observe everything closely. Attentiveness to detail saves lives."

"Ah. Like you observed my failure to keep myself adequately fed."

Holsworth made a sort of scraping noise in his throat, and the vibration of it ran through the bracelet into her wrist. "That observation wasn't meant as an insult, Lady Grantleigh," he said. "It was—merely an expression of concern for your well-being."

"Was it? I don't know a single lady who wouldn't take umbrage at being called *too thin*."

It was absurd, of course, to banter with him like this. But she had no other bulwark against the discomfort of their situation. "In fact," she continued, "some ladies would go into a decline at hearing such a thing, and never show their faces, or their figures, in society again."

Holsworth went very still, and she could make out just enough in the dim glow of moonlight to tell that he was staring hard at her. "You never struck me as that kind of woman," he said.

"As what kind of woman?"

"Trivial. Vain." His voice darkened, seemed to drop half an octave. "Unaware of your true value."

Oh. He was still staring at her, and suddenly bantering didn't seem like a safe thing to be doing, at all.

Thank goodness he looked away, back at the recalcitrant bracelet. "I seem to be well and truly caught," he said a moment later, as irritably as before. "I thought the clasp was lodged in the braid of my coat, but it seems actually to have got onto the underside of the lapel somehow, and heaven knows how badly the other side of it is tangled in my shirt. Can you slide your hand out? The weight of your arm is only making things worse."

She clucked her tongue at him. "Making things *worse*? You know, Major Holsworth, gentlemen are meant to *compliment* ladies. First you call me too thin, and now you make me sound like an awkward lump of flesh. I fear your manners have taken a turn for the worse in your time away from England."

"Have they?" he said dryly. "I thought you were of the opinion that I was never in possession of manners at all."

Oh. Was he joking with her? Or was he genuinely offended?

Good Lord, was he *aware* she'd always disliked him?

He breathed out an impatient sigh. "You never did approve of me, did you?"

Well, that took care of that question as well.

It was *he* who'd first disapproved of her, of course. But even so, if she'd been so indiscreet as to let her feelings about him show, it was time to make amends.

"You were my husband's dearest friend," she assured him, schooling her voice to graciousness again. "Christopher respected you as he respected no one else in the world. And I would never gainsay his judgment."

Holsworth gave a dark laugh. "A suitably equivocal thing to say. Your *husband* always respected me. And of course a proper lady would never refute the word of her lord, no matter how sharply her private opinion might diverge. Your manners are, as always, exquisite, Lady Grantleigh."

Well, then. Holsworth was rather more nimble at this bantering business than she'd given him credit for. He'd managed to shut her mouth entirely, for the moment at least.

"Come now," he said abruptly. "We must get into the light, or I'll never get this blasted bauble of yours unhooked."

Blasted bauble? *That* helped her find her tongue again. "It's your blasted clothing that's hooked my bauble." It was a silly retort, and by no means a proper one, but she found it was strangely refreshing to speak so tartly. How long had it been since she'd teased or joked with anyone?

Oh, she knew—she knew exactly. *Eighteen months.*

Since Christopher had been taken from her.

That Major Holsworth, of all people, should spark the

habit in her again was rather painfully ironic. But she couldn't seem to stop herself.

"Besides," she heard herself saying, "why should I follow you anywhere? You haven't yet explained why you were skulking about in the darkness in the first place."

His shadowed outline stiffened. "I never *skulk*, Lady Grantleigh," he said. "I am merely unaccustomed to the frenzy of society ballrooms, and withdrew a moment to admire the moonlight."

"We're in the wilds of Devon, sir. Ballrooms here are hardly frenzied."

"Compared to the wilds of India, ma'am, your ballroom is frenzied indeed. And I might point out that you yourself were doing some skulking."

Her chin jutted forward. "I wasn't skulking. I live here."

"Fair enough. In that case, you might know of a reasonably private space where I could actually *see* to disentangle us. If you could lead us there, I'd be most grateful."

Ah, yes. Disentanglement was, of course, the goal.

If they stood here much longer, all but entwined, someone was sure to come upon them and think they were in the midst of a scandalous romantic rendezvous.

"There's—there's a sitting room just a little way behind us," she said. "Hidden behind that stand of date palms. It's built just over the boiler, to take advantage of the heat."

"Good," Holsworth said, his deep voice rough. "Since this might require removal of my coat."

Her heart skipped a beat, or perhaps tried to perform several beats at once. She swallowed hard. "Removal of ...your *coat*?"

Well, they certainly couldn't let anyone else be witness to that. As far as the sticklers of Society were concerned, a gentleman showing his shirtsleeves to a lady was tantamount to stripping nude.

"Unfortunately," he said, "that damnable bracelet's snagged between my coat and my linen in some maddeningly complicated way."

Maddeningly complicated. Yes, that phrase seemed apt at the moment.

For the man as well as the predicament.

And for her own mood, too. She was irritated, frustrated, of course, by the absurdity of the situation, but also somehow…*buoyant.*

I am almost enjoying this.

Not a thought she wanted to consider in detail.

Thankfully, Holsworth got things moving. He set one large hand to the small of her back, and wrapped the other about her trapped wrist, presumably to keep the bracelet from ripping at his clothing as they walked.

Or perhaps to spare pressure on her arm. It might even be…*courtly* of him, she supposed. Considerate, at least. Perhaps even protective.

Despite his sometimes primitive manners, the man seemed more than capable of protecting a woman.

A realization which sent a peculiar flutter through her middle.

To her relief, he released her wrist to open the sitting room door, usher her inside, and throw the bolt shut for privacy. But then he made the fluttering worse by reaching across her to feel for the silver tinderbox that was always kept on a little table by the entrance.

And then it occurred to her that he'd been teasing before: he knew perfectly well this room was here. After all, he'd grown up in this house. Had in fact spent more years in it than she had.

A maddeningly complicated man, indeed.

Both hands were needed to strike the flint, so he all but embraced her as he knocked sparks from flint and steel and puffed a breath to make the wood splint flare. He tipped the burning splint into the lantern beside the tinderbox, so neatly he scarcely rattled the glass, and the candle-wick hissed into flame.

Now a golden circle of light surrounded them.

And, oh, she wished they were still lost in darkness.

The sight of him, so very close, was after all far more disconcerting than being with him in the darkness. His bulk was intimidating enough when just a looming shadow, but now it had depth and dimension and color that made her all the more conscious he was genuine flesh and blood.

And, Lord, she'd never paid attention to the shape of Holsworth's mouth before, to the generous sweep of his lower lip.

Or to how striking his dark eyes were, with their black fringe of lashes.

Christopher had been so fair, his hair nearly as silken as a child's and his pale scalp visible along his part, but Holsworth's hair was thick and dark as night, its waves so dense she couldn't tell if he parted it at all.

And then of course there was that frightening scar…

The warmth of his breath mingling with hers suddenly made her almost too self-conscious to take in another lungful of air.

Holsworth seemed to be studying her face, too, his body unnaturally still, his gaze intense but impenetrable in its intentions. She felt it like pressure against her skin—and had the disconcerting sensation that she was being stroked with black velvet.

A flush of heat ran up her throat.

Perhaps he noticed the color come into her cheeks, because he looked away suddenly, grasping her wrist again almost roughly. "Let me get a proper look at that bracelet," he said.

With the metal snagged near his collarbone, he had to crane his neck awkwardly, and he twisted her wrist back and forth to get a look at the closures. His eyes widened suddenly, and his gaze snapped back to hers. "Where did you get this?"

His tone was sharp, almost accusing, and his fingers closed tighter on her arm.

"Why do you ask?" *And what business is it of yours?* Her pulse was growing more rapid again. Did he recognize the bracelet after all?

"It's from India," he said harshly, and it seemed to be a statement and a question all at once.

"It is," she confirmed, refusing to let her discomposure show on her face. After all, she was under no obligation to tell him that she herself had no more information about the bracelet than that. "How did you know?"

"The color of the gold—a purer alloy than Europeans use. And the inscription appears to be in Sanskrit."

"Yes," she said. "Do you know what it says?"

He hesitated. "I can't see enough of it to tell. In any case, I'm no scholar. Urdu and Marathi are of more use to army officers."

Christopher was a scholar. That thought went through her with a pang.

Oh, why was she here with this piratical soldier and not with her gentle husband? Why should the man who'd spent years having bullets fired at him be alive, while the one who'd sat safely behind a desk have perished? The universe made no sense at all.

And why on earth could she not stop feeling so conscious of the heat and size of Holsworth's body, of that disquieting exotic scent of his, of the dark tinge of stubble along his jaw?

This excessive awareness of him was merely the reaction of her flesh, to be sure. For all these months since Christopher died, she'd lived in dreams and shadows, lying in her cold bed alone at night. She'd barely remembered she had a body.

And Holsworth was certainly very *bodily*.

So large and strong and irrefutably *male*. So vital, she fancied she could hear his heart pulsing, the blood rushing beneath the surface of his skin.

Suddenly the thought of him putting his arms around her, of him putting his mouth against hers, began to beat at the back of her skull like a drum.

Thankfully, Holsworth, for his part, now seemed focused entirely on practical matters. He had his chin down, squinting at the bracelet again. "Where is this pin you mentioned? To release the clasp?"

She had to feel for the tiny metal nub herself, her knuckles brushing the underside of Holsworth's jaw and pressing into his uniform front as she searched. Goodness, the man was hard as a rock, everywhere.

Holsworth could probably snap her in two if he wanted. And judging from the harsh expression on his face just now, she wasn't entirely sure he didn't want to.

There—her fingertip found the pin at last. She pressed her nail into the tip as she had the first time, and waited for the front seam to pop open.

It didn't pop.

She pressed once more.

Still nothing.

"It—it's not working."

"Damnation," he swore. "You must have damaged the mechanism in the fall."

"*I* must have damaged it? May I remind you that you *knocked me down*. Deliberately, I might add. And you still haven't explained why."

He blew out an impatient breath. "I thought you were— oh, never mind what I thought."

She planted her one free fist on her hip. "In any case, it was *your* weight that struck the bracelet, not mine! I merely struck the floor."

He swore again—a word she wasn't familiar with, and which might not be English at all, but uttered in the unmistakable tone of male obscenity.

"Are you certain you can't just pull your hand out?" he asked, gripping her wrist with thumb and forefinger as though he were about to force the issue himself.

"Stop that!" she snapped. "If I were capable of pulling my hand through, don't you think I'd have done it by now?"

"Well, I can't seem to get the fabric free," he said, as though that were somehow her fault. "It looks like part of my shirt is caught inside that little separation where you say the clasp is. And the inside of my lapel's caught in the seam on the other side. It's like the bloody thing bit down on me, on purpose."

She laughed. "You're attributing malevolent intention to my bracelet?"

"You explain it."

"You're big as a bull," she said bluntly. "Your weight probably forced the two sides apart just long enough to wedge the fabric inside. And they closed up again when—when you got up again. And now it's jammed somehow."

She didn't feel as though they were bantering anymore. Merely being quite direct with one another. But it was strange—as uncomfortable as she felt with him in so many ways, she also felt more at ease in his presence than she ever had when they were actually trying to be civil. *Necessity makes strange bedfellows*, she thought. And instantly regretted the image that brought into her mind.

"Big as a bull, eh?" he said, musing, his voice oddly softer than before. "That I am, I'm afraid." His gaze met hers again, steadily, and now his brow creased with concern. "Good

Lord—I didn't hurt you, Lady Grantleigh, did I, when I knocked you down? I suppose I should have asked you that much earlier than this. Beg pardon. I've spent my adult life disabling enemies, not inquiring after their welfare."

Again, she laughed. "Enemies? Do you count me among their number?"

To her shock, a tinge of ruddy color appeared on his cheeks.

"No. Never," he said. "Of course not." Lord, his eyes were so very black, almost unfathomable. And somehow, as deep as they were, their gaze seemed to reach far inside of her, too. "You must know, Lady Grantleigh," he said softly, "you are everything admirable."

Oh. She wasn't at all sure what to say to that. The flesh prickled all along her arms, and along the fronts of her legs.

Standing close to him had been far easier to manage when he was being harsh with her.

"On your wedding day," he said, just as softly, his eyes still boring into hers, "do you know what Christopher asked of me?"

"No," she whispered.

"He asked me to protect you, and look after you, if ever he could not." His gaze sharpened, somehow, and he seemed about to say something even more profound. But then his mouth pursed, and his eyes slanted back down at the bracelet again. His tone became lighter, ironic. "And look what a fine job I'm doing of it."

The joke did nothing to lighten the strange tension that gripped her. *Christopher had asked him to protect her?*

The oddest sensation twinged in the center of her chest.

The sheer power of the man seemed palpable, pressing down against her.

And, then, for some reason, the image of the carved dancing girl atop the jewel box came into her mind, the silky-looking cloth about her hips, the pearls draped over her bare breasts. And Julia's own breasts seemed to tighten.

Good Lord. She really did have to dispel this strange mood that was taking her over, or the next thing she knew, she'd be thinking dangerous thoughts about Major Holsworth taking off his coat, and perhaps his shirt as well, and she'd be wondering what that huge, hard body of his looked like when it was stripped bare.

She gave her head a little shake. "Oh, please, Major," she said, trying to keep her tone nonchalant. "Don't be so serious about things. What's happened here was a silly accident, nothing more. Something to laugh over one day."

He nodded gravely. "I'm glad to hear you have that attitude," he said, "because it's about to get worse."

A peculiar thrill raced down her spine at his words. "*Worse*? In what way worse?"

"If the pin on your bracelet won't work, and you can't slide your wrist through, there's no help for it, Lady Grantleigh." He drew a rather ragged breath. "I'm going to have to start disrobing."

CHAPTER 3

*W*atching Julia's mouth form a perfect *O*, Marcus immediately regretted his choice of words.

Blast it. Look at her, standing so stiff, her trapped wrist bent back painfully to keep her fingers from touching him. Clearly, she'd rather greet her morning callers in her undergarments than be entangled like this with him.

His stomach roiled. If she was this uncomfortable with him now, how was she going to react when he told her the *real* reason for his return to England? When he told her about the danger he'd unwittingly put her in?

That mess would be hard enough to explain when he could sit her down and talk through it soberly. When she could slap his face and storm out of the room if she wanted to.

He wasn't about to attempt it now, while they were latched together like this.

He gave the bracelet one last desperate pull, digging a thumbnail into the tiny crease that hid the clasp. The damned thing still wouldn't budge.

Well, there was no help for it. He had to get them both unstuck, and as quickly as possible. For the sake of his own sanity. He had far too many complicated feelings about this woman to be this close to her for much longer.

"I beg your pardon most sincerely," he said, gripping the top gold button of his coat. "But I see no other option." He plucked the button free, and moved on to the next.

Julia's shoulders flinched slightly with each one he undid.

Damn it all. Was his physical presence really so horrifying to her?

Old resentments pricked at him, resentments that weren't normally among the discomforts Julia had ever made him feel. War hero or not, most members of her class never forgot he was a farmer's son, and regarded him as though a whiff of cow dung always trailed in his wake.

Most of the time, he shrugged off their snobbery. Since his first days at Cambridge, he'd proved again and again and again that he could beat the soft sons of the aristocracy at any game, any task, any fight they were foolish enough to challenge him to.

But *Julia* shrinking from him—that hurt more than he cared to admit.

Of course, modesty alone could account for her discomfort. A man should keep his coat on in the presence of a lady, and Julia was a lady of the highest order.

He clenched his jaw and freed another button. And Julia visibly trembled.

"So," she said, eyes averted somewhere off to his left, her voice pitched unusually high. "Tell me, Major Holsworth. What exactly brings you back to Devon?"

His eyebrows lifted. "Are we making polite conversation now?" Even to his own ears, his tone sounded unreasonably harsh.

"I believe it would make this situation easier, yes."

31

This situation. He blew out a breath of frustration. "My reasons for returning to Devon wouldn't make for easy discussion, believe me."

At that, Julia's gaze flicked back to meet his, and her rigid shoulders softened. "That sounds ominous," she said. And, to make matters worse, her eyes brightened with sudden concern. For *him.* "Is everything all right, Major Holsworth?" she asked. "Are you—are you in trouble of some kind?"

Oh.

Oh, yes, he was in trouble. Very deep trouble.

And it had nothing to do with her bracelet, or snobbery, or even the threat he'd learned about in India.

The real trouble had to do with her *eyes.*

Because every time she looked at him, the room began to spin.

Damnation. If only he'd stayed in India from the very first time he'd traveled there, and never set foot on English soil again. Never met Julia at all. Because all the trouble in his life started on the fateful day he first saw her.

Back when they met, she was still Lady Julia, not yet Lady Grantleigh. Belle of the London Season, the only daughter of the wealthy, powerful Earl of Allendale—and Christopher's newly sworn betrothed.

Christopher had been so eager to introduce his beloved to his best friend, he'd sent letters begging Marcus to take leave from the army in India and travel home, and even met Marcus's ship at the wharf to bring him straight to the Allendale town house. Chris was clearly floating on clouds, and for the short ride through the London streets, Marcus found the situation quite amusing—his ever-capable, always brilliant friend struck into utter stupidity by Cupid's arrow.

"I know you will adore her," Christopher had sighed, slumping bonelessly against the leather squabs, an imbecilic grin on his face, and Marcus had to bite his own lip to suppress laughter. Aside from resisting the urge to mock his friend, the biggest challenge he thought he'd face for the rest of his leave was feigning interest in the chatter of whatever insipid seventeen-year-old miss had managed to bewitch the young earl's heart.

But nothing could have prepared him for Lady Julia.

For Christopher had been entirely correct: Marcus *did* adore her.

Marcus had always been a logical man. He made practical choices. Controlled himself. But meeting Julia was, as all the poets said, like being thunderstruck.

When a footman ushered them into Lord Allendale's foyer, Julia came hurrying down the grand staircase to greet her fiancé. Marcus's first impression was innocuous enough: a lovely girl in a white muslin frock, with a heart-shaped face and shining dark curls, a perfectly proper bride for an illustrious peer like the young Earl of Grantleigh. And not at all the sort of mate for a coarse soldier like himself.

But just as Julia passed through the afternoon light streaming from the foyer window, she looked up and met Marcus's eyes. And everything changed.

It was as though he'd been sleepwalking all his life, and was instantly shocked awake. Those eyes of hers, so remarkably blue, seemed lit from within, as fierce and pure as lightning. A hot jolt blasted straight through his skull down to the soles of his boots.

And the shock hadn't stopped reverberating since.

No physical torture could have been worse. The girl was already wooed and won by *Christopher*—his closest friend in all the world, his sworn brother, a man he'd have died to protect. And yet, one evening, when Marcus came upon the couple just as Christopher was stealing a kiss from his soon-to-be countess, it was all Marcus could do not to throw

Christopher bodily away from her and slam a fist through his teeth.

For the first week or so, Marcus thought—he *hoped*—it was only Julia's beauty that had struck him such a blow. That would have made sense, and been manageable, because she *was* beautiful, startlingly so, with the natural sweetness of her features, the grace of her movements, her smooth white shoulders and her slender waist. Even her voice was alluring, low and musical, with a delicious undertone of laughter.

A purely physical attraction he could have handled, once the initial impact wore off. He was a military man. He knew how to deny the needs of the body.

But, as he realized all too quickly, it was something else entirely that drew him to her. That light in her eyes truly came from within—she was bright and quick and clever, and though he did his best to be gruff and standoffish with her, and though he knew he rather terrified her, she made every effort to include him in conversation, to make him feel his presence was wanted, to make him believe he fit into her rarified world.

Lightning, it turned out, wasn't at all the right analogy for the brightness of her gaze. What shone from her eyes was *sunlight*—warm and life-giving and generous, everything he'd lost the day he was orphaned as a boy. She made him crave things he'd spent years training himself not to want: intimacy, coming first in someone's affections, a sense of belonging fully.

It was painful to feel it. His throat pinched tight and his chest ached whenever Lady Julia was near.

His chest ached now.

Steeling himself, he freed another button on his coat. The weight of his lapel sagged, pulling Julia's wrist with it, and also pulling at the top of his shirt. With the collar held tight within the stiff circle of his stock, the extra tension against his throat made him almost light-headed.

"Oh, I can see where it's snagged you now," said Julia. "It really has got your coat and linen both—one bit on each side."

"Can you pull it loose?"

Her cheeks pinkened further, but she reached her free hand to the level of his collarbone and gave his linen a hard tug. Once more, and then again. It did no more good than all the pulling he'd done earlier.

"I'm sorry," she said. "There's too little room to get my fingers between the bracelet and your collar. Perhaps it would help if—if you removed your stock."

Her blush went full scarlet as soon as she said the words.

Good heavens. The sight of a few square inches of shirt unnerved her, and now the prospect of glimpsing his bare throat had her looking quite ready to swoon. She'd been a married woman for more than six years—shouldn't she be a bit less skittish than this around a man's body?

Then again, he suspected his own color must be up as well—the sight of her cheeks going rosy had his blood pounding almost savagely, making his jaw throb. Damn it all. Why hadn't all those years in the blazing Indian sun burnt these feelings for her out of him?

"Get on with it," Julia said, in the sort of tone men used when bound before a firing squad. "And find an acceptable topic of conversation to distract us in the meanwhile, if you please."

He clenched his teeth against the odd pulse of tenderness her imperious tone made him feel. "All right," he said, reaching behind his neck to unbuckle the heavy black band of his stock. "Here's an interesting topic: where did you get the bracelet?"

Her eyes shot to his again, sparking their brilliant blue. "That's none of your business."

Damn those eyes of hers.

He wasn't going to think how easy it would be, with her so close, to steal a kiss of his own. He *wasn't*. Her marriage to Christopher had truly been a sacred bond, and it would be sacrilege to muddy its purity.

Besides, any relationship between himself and Julia could only meet with Society's scorn. He'd been born in the dirt, and he couldn't imagine dragging her down there with him.

With a growl, he pulled at the end piece of his stock, and the prong of the buckle popped loose. The release of pressure was a relief, and the veins of his neck gave a grateful throb—though without the stiff band holding his shirt closed, the weight of Julia's arm made the collar gape wide, exposing not just his neck but a goodly part of his chest as well.

Julia sucked in an audible breath. "Please suggest another subject for conversation," she demanded, her voice tight. "*Immediately.*"

What on earth was he to say to her?

He knew what he needed to say, but he'd already spent the voyage from India trying and failing to find a decent way to say it.

I believe an old friend of your husband's may have turned traitor in India. Christopher refused to heed my warnings, and now Christopher is dead. And the evidence I left with him may draw the villain here to your home, in hopes of permanently concealing his crimes. So I may have put your life in danger, too.

No. He couldn't possibly say all that now.

Not while he needed every ounce of discipline he possessed to resist pulling Julia into his arms.

She risked a brief glance up at him. "Tell me about India," she said with forced brightness, as though that would be a safe topic. "Tell me what your latest victory means.

Peace at last, isn't that so? The stable government Christopher worked so hard for?"

Oh, Lord. She certainly had a knack for making this situation ever more uncomfortable for him. "It seems so," he answered.

Her brow furrowed. "Only seems?"

"No, not seems—the government *is* in firm control. And shall be for quite a long time to come."

She cocked her head to one side, regarding him curiously. "But you sound less than enthusiastic about that success."

He hesitated before answering. "To be honest, Lady Grantleigh, the longer I've been in India, the more I've wondered whether Britain has any business being there at all."

"But the British restored the national government!" She looked stunned by his comment. "Before we arrived, India had splintered into warring kingdoms. It was chaos!"

Ah, she'd learned those words from her husband. Chris never questioned the righteousness of the British cause. But then again, Chris had never set foot in India.

"Is Europe so very different?" Marcus asked. "Our kingdoms are often at war, but would you prefer to have an outside power step in and unite us?"

"Well, I…" Julia's color deepened once more, this time at least not from embarrassment. "I don't believe Europe is in need of such interference."

"Is India? India was a great civilization a thousand years before Europe stopped burning witches."

She stared at him for several long seconds, and he could almost see the struggle going on inside her mind. His words must sound like heresy to her. Dear God, he needed to get this bracelet unhooked and get away from her before he said or did something she'd never forgive him for.

"Did you ever share these views with Christopher?" Julia asked at last.

"Yes," he admitted. "The last time we were together."

Strangely enough, she nodded. She looked almost relieved. "So that's what you argued about."

She *knew* he and Christopher had argued? Surely Chris hadn't told her everything they'd argued over, or she'd have more questions for him now. About Brayles, about why Marcus had now returned to Devon so unexpectedly. And he truly wasn't ready for that conversation just yet.

"The stock's off," he said abruptly. "Why don't you try again to pull your bracelet loose?"

"Oh," she said, blinking. "Yes, of course."

Dutifully, she took hold of the frilled edge of his collar, though her fingers shook and her blush was furious again. A flurry of emotions assaulted him as he watched her—relief that she hadn't pushed him any harder with her questions about India, a longing to press his mouth to hers, and another strange, aching, vulnerable feeling he didn't even know how to name.

And then suddenly, sharply, he found himself missing *Christopher*.

It came on all at once, in a hard wave, the way it had so many times since he'd first learned the awful news—the memory of Christopher's decency, his unflinching desire to do what was right, the cruelty of a fate that would take the life of such a good-hearted man so young.

And now he could add to that the sheer wrongness of Grantleigh Hall without its proper master.

Of course, as always, that sharp grief was mixed with a terrible weight of guilt. For…far too many things.

Now Julia's knuckles rubbed against his throat and chest as she struggled to work his shirt free of the bracelet's clasp. She shot him an apologetic look. "I *am* trying to free it," she said. "The cloth's terribly snarled. And wedged in tight. I don't understand how that tiny seam in the bracelet could have opened wide enough to capture so much of it."

He forced his attention to the bracelet, not the woman. With his collar loosened, he could now twist his neck at enough of an angle to see the inscription in full. The script was indeed Devanagari, and the language Sanskrit. He had to decipher the letters upside down, but at least it was a distraction from the other thoughts careening about inside his head.

He was expecting a name, perhaps, or words of dedication from a gift-giver. Instead the engraving looked to be two lines of classical Sanskrit verse.

"That's peculiar," he said.

"What's peculiar?"

"The inscription on your bracelet. I believe it may be…" He squinted at the swirling script, running through the grammar again to be sure he wasn't mistaken. "It seems to be some sort of *riddle*."

"A riddle?" Julia's eyes fixed on the lettering, and she inclined her head closer to his chest, so close he could smell a hint of lavender in her hair. "What on earth does it say?"

He attempted to translate without inhaling again—her hands touching his chest muddled his thoughts enough without her scent fuming through his brain. "The first line says, *Gold cannot buy me, I must be found.*"

Julia gasped, and her eyes went wide. "*I must be found?* Is that what it really says?"

"Yes."

"*I must be found,*" she murmured again, as though something about those words was particularly intriguing.

"Indeed, it does seem a rather odd claim. *Gold cannot buy me?* The thing's *made* of gold—and precisely the sort of thing people spend their money on. And not something they generally leave laying about for others to find."

Julia ignored his comment. "And what about the second line?"

He paused, puzzling over the next bit once more. Something about the rhythm of the words struck him as familiar, though he couldn't quite put his finger on why. As for the meaning, he came up with nothing more coherent than he had on his first reading. He sighed. "I believe it says, *I am yours forever when you give me away.*"

"*Yours forever*?" she echoed back. "*When you give me away*?"

"Indeed. A blatant contradiction in terms. Hence, a riddle of some sort." Frankly, the nonsense of the words irritated his logical military mind.

But Julia was breathing rather alarmingly fast, and her cheeks went pale.

He frowned. "Are you quite all right, Lady Grantleigh?"

"Yes," she said, nodding abstractedly, and waved the fingers of her free hand. "Yes, I'm fine."

"I wouldn't ponder it too seriously," he advised. "To be honest, the whole thing sounds like blather to me—some bit of mysticism a goldsmith thought would catch the fancy of a suggestible client." He gave the bracelet another futile tug. "I wish we *could* give the blasted thing away. If it wants so badly to be set loose, it shouldn't grip hold with such tenacity."

Julia stared off into the distance. "*Yours forever,*" she repeated yet again, a strange edge in her voice. "*When you give me away*?"

"Yes. Does that mean something to you?"

She didn't answer. She pressed her free hand over her mouth and—good Lord—were those *tears* forming in her eyes?

Clearly, the words triggered strong emotion in her. Was she upset?

Frightened?

When she'd asked him earlier if he could read the inscription, she'd seemed genuinely ignorant of what it said. And the bracelet was clearly quite old, the engraving done at least a century before Julia was born. The message—if it *was* a message, and not just a fatuous bit of balderdash—couldn't possibly have been intended for her.

So why was it affecting her so strongly?

"Do you—do you understand the meaning of these phrases, Lady Grantleigh?" His mind began to race through disturbing possibilities. Had that villain Brayles somehow managed to reach this house before he did? Had the treacherous bastard somehow been in contact with Julia already? *Threatened* her with similar words?

Had the bracelet somehow come from him?

"It's nothing," Julia said, tears still welling.

The muscles of Marcus's body hardened into knots. "Tell me," he insisted. "Tell me this instant."

Julia glanced at him, clearly confused by his harsh tone, and began to draw herself up straight in resistance again. But she must have seen the genuine anxiety in his expression, because after a moment, she relented. "Oh, well," she said, sighing. "You'll think me foolish, Major, no doubt. But I—I *did* find the bracelet."

"You what?"

"I found it. In my—my private chamber." She was blushing again, unaccountably. "Just this evening."

"*Found* it?" Damn it all. Brayles hadn't found a way to enter her *home*, had he? Without her knowledge? Entered her *bedchamber*? Marcus should have ripped the traitor's head from his shoulders when he first began to suspect his involvement with the Pindaris.

Julia's eyes widened—no doubt his expression had turned ferocious.

"I never saw the bracelet before tonight," she hurried to

say. "I swear. It was just *there*. In a box. On the hearth." Tears shone in her eyes again, and she sucked at her lower lip. "Someone—someone must have left it for me. I thought…"

"What?" he demanded, rather more forcefully than he intended. "You thought what?"

"Well, I—I thought for a moment it might have been—" She broke off on a sob. "I thought it was—it was *Christopher* who left it. Somehow." Twin tears spilled now and rolled down her cheeks. "I know that's terribly foolish."

Oh, dear Lord. *I am the world's most brainless ass.*

Julia wasn't upset because of any threat from Brayles.

She was upset because she missed her husband desperately.

I am yours forever—no wonder those words affected her so powerfully, if she believed they might be a message from her beloved beyond the grave.

Marcus wanted to kick himself. He was too used to thinking tactically, like a soldier, not like a civilian. While Julia had lived all her life in the domestic sphere, in a world centered on her loving marriage.

Once he took Brayles out of the equation, the solution to the mystery came to him immediately, and there was nothing either sinister or supernatural about the business.

The bracelet *was* a gift, and it *was* brought from India, and it *was* in fact given with affection. But it must have been *Lady Eleanor* who'd slipped it into Julia's room.

Of course it was her. Christopher's Aunt Eleanor, who meant no harm to anyone, who no doubt found the bracelet's verses intriguing, in some sentimental, poetical way.

But, great heavens, what had the old woman been thinking, to leave a surprise gift for her nephew's widow like that, when poor Julia didn't even know Christopher's aunt was back in the country? Surely Lady Eleanor must have understood that a mysteriously appearing bracelet would alarm Lady Grantleigh. Even for Eleanor, who never met a rule she wished to obey, it was an oddly thoughtless impulse.

And now Marcus had a weeping woman to comfort.

Bloody hell. His talents were in fending off rampaging bandits and enemy cannon fire, not a lady's tears.

"Lady Grantleigh," he said tentatively, laying a hand on her shoulder.

Damn it all, why were the sleeves of women's ball gowns so flimsy and diaphanous? His fingers touched far too much warm, soft skin for the good of his composure, and he felt an answering wave of heat shoot through him.

Heat he very definitely had to ignore.

He removed his hand. "I believe I know how that bracelet found its way into your room."

Julia gave a sudden jolt, and she went pink again. "*You* know?"

"Yes. Well, I wasn't meant to reveal this to you. It was meant to be a surprise. But—the truth is, I didn't return from India alone."

"You...*what?*"

"Christopher's aunt, Lady Eleanor, traveled with me." He didn't have to tell Julia the rest of the surprise. Eleanor could hold her other, more startling, news in store.

Julia stared up at him, mouth agape, blinking away her tears. "Aunt Eleanor's come home again? From India? But—she sent no word!"

"She wished to astonish you with her sudden arrival, but when we pulled up to the house and discovered a party underway..." He trailed off, not wanting to reveal more than he had to. Perhaps a small white lie would not hurt in this case. "Well, I believe the fatigue of travel convinced her to conceal herself and rest till morning. But it seems she couldn't resist astonishing you in the meantime—with that bracelet."

"Eleanor?" Julia repeated, her voice gone oddly flat. "Aunt *Eleanor* left the bracelet for me?"

He shrugged. "I don't actually know for certain. But if you don't know the origin of the gift, the most plausible explanation is that she put it in your room."

"Oh." The color was rapidly draining from Julia's cheeks, and her shoulders sagged. "That—that makes sense. Perfect sense. Of course. If Aunt Eleanor's come home from India, she must have put the bracelet there."

Blast it. Marcus had a sudden feeling he ought to be apologizing. He'd thought a rational explanation for the appearance of the bracelet would relieve Julia's distress, but somehow it only dimmed her spirits.

And that seemed far worse than the tears.

Earlier, when he'd told Julia she'd grown too thin, it wasn't just the sharper cut of her cheekbones or the new fragility in her wrists that made him speak. It was the muting of her inner light, the veil that seemed to have been drawn over the brightness of her eyes—the look of mourning, which persisted despite the cornflower-colored gown she wore.

The change in her had made him want to weep.

Now an urge to move, to take action, pumped through him, but the only action that seemed possible under the circumstances was, at long last, liberating the snagged bracelet.

So, with no other options at his disposal, he released the last button of his coat and writhed his shoulders until he was able to wrench his arms from his tightly tailored sleeves, not caring if half the seams were rent, but taking care not to jerk Julia's wrist too hard. He might not be able to do much for her, but at least he could get his damned coat off.

It was indecent, but it worked.

With his arms out, the bulk of the coat slipped off his back, and for just one moment, the whole weight of it hung suspended from Julia's wrist. The coat was heavy—heavy enough to pull Julia's fist hard against his chest. For a moment, it seemed that weight might snap the bracelet in two.

But then, miracle of miracles, the bracelet let go its stubborn grip on the lapel, and the coat slumped free to the floor.

"Look!" cried Julia, a bit more energy in her tone. "It's spit your coat out, finally!"

Ah—progress, at least. He'd made that happen for her.

He drew a quick breath. "Maybe it will go the same with my shirt." He didn't stop to think it through. He made quick work of removing his waistcoat, then grabbed one cuff of his shirt in the opposite fist and yanked his arm from the sleeve, seized the hem and drew the whole thing up over his head.

The collar, of course, was still attached to the bracelet on Julia's wrist, so the shirt tented partway over her head as he tossed the hem away from him. But he was unfettered now, and could move more than a few inches away from her, which he was sorely, sorely in need of doing.

She batted her way free of the pool of linen, coming out with her hair a bit mussed and her cheeks pinker again—and the shirt now hanging down from her bracelet like a miniature sail unfurled from a mast.

She gave her arm three hard shakes, and on the third, the shirt popped loose from the clasp at last and billowed its way to the floor beside his coat.

"Thank God!" he exclaimed.

But Julia, for her part, didn't seem inclined to celebrate. She stared at the pile of his clothing for a moment, then doubled over with a sudden keening noise, gripping her knees with her hands. Her back was convulsing.

Was she...having a fit of some sort? Was she choking?

He was halfway through rushing back over to her and seizing her about the shoulders when he realized she was *laughing*. He stopped dead.

"Oh, that is absurd," she said, straightening partway again, and wiping at fresh tears with the heel of her hand. "Utterly absurd. It was stuck so tight."

"Well," he said, quite dumbfounded. "Well...I...the weight of the fabric. It must have pulled in just the right way, once it was hanging down."

She shook her head firmly. "Oh, no—don't try logic, Major Holsworth. Logic doesn't apply tonight."

"No?" Since when did logic not apply to everything?

"No. It doesn't apply in the slightest. " She looked up at him, still laughing, and her eyes were oddly bright. "And I have no interest in more of your *plausible explanations*. You see, I understand it all now."

"You—you *do*?"

"Oh, yes. It's quite obvious."

"What's obvious?"

"It's obvious," she said, smiling, "that I've gone mad."

"*What*?"

"Mad," she declared calmly. "Completely mad. Stark raving."

CHAPTER 4

"*Mad?*" His stomach dropped to his boots. "Lady Grantleigh, you—you're not—"

She dismissed his objection with an imperious wave of her fingers. "Oh, but madness would explain so much," she said. "*You* here, for one thing, appearing in our ballroom in Devon, when clearly you should still be in India."

"As I said, I—"

"And Eleanor, sneaking into the house after traveling so very far, not showing her face, but leaving a *bracelet* in my room. What sort of nonsense is that?" Her voice became almost enthusiastic as she warmed to her topic. Able to move freely now, she began to make a little circuit of the room, her skirts swishing about her heels. "And more ridiculously still, the bracelet *latching* itself onto one of your garments, no, *two* of your garments, as though by deliberate will. You said yourself it seemed to have conscious intent, and inanimate objects are not generally supposed to be capable of that."

His jaw didn't seem to be working quite right. "I'm—I'm sure there's a perfectly rational—"

"And that's not to mention you *tackling* me in the conservatory. You've been unmannerly to me occasionally in the past, but *nothing* on that level of incivility."

"Oh!" He racked his brain for an easy way to explain his actions, but anything he could think to say to her about Brayles would only add to the list of absurdities. "Well, I—"

"Ha! You *can't* explain it!" She came to a standstill, crossing her arms over her chest, looking almost triumphant. "Clearly, then, I'm asleep and dreaming all this, or it's lunacy. Either way, it's a grand hallucination. Much more entertaining than anything that's happened to me in months."

Marcus gaped at her. Was she being serious? Julia had always had a lively sense of humor, but he wished he could be sure she was joking with him now.

Her eyes squeezed shut, then, and she heaved a shaky breath, the laughter dying on her lips. "Oh, perhaps Aunt Margaret was right," she said. "Perhaps I stayed in my widow's blacks too long. Or perhaps—it wasn't long enough. Perhaps I shouldn't have given them up at all." The next breath was rather more like a sob. "I think that must be it."

"What…must be it?"

"The dark, heavy color," she said. "And all that weighty bombazine. It was an anchor of sorts, I suppose. In these past months, these *awful* months. " Her fingers plucked fretfully at the frothy blue silk of her skirts. "I didn't want to give up my mourning clothes, but I did, and now I've—I've snapped my tether. I've gone adrift."

It certainly didn't sound like she was joking now.

But she didn't sound like a madwoman, either. Her words were sensible enough.

Just *sad*.

No…worse than sad. *Heartbroken*.

Of course she was. It didn't take logic to tell him that.

But what on earth was he to do or say? He wanted to go to her and put his arms around her, but he suspected that

48

would only upset her more—especially since he was no longer wearing a shirt.

He'd have to try to manage it with words.

"You haven't gone mad," he said, taking care to make his voice gentle and soft.

She sniffled. "Haven't I?"

He supposed logic wasn't really what she needed right now, but logic was all that came to him. "I assure you, everything that's happened tonight is quite real, however odd it all seems. In any case, I know I am no phantasm."

She laughed again, and he was relieved to hear a note of genuine humor in it. "Oh, please! You're the best evidence I have that this is all a dream."

"Am I?"

"*Look* at you!" she exclaimed, her manner becoming almost giddy, like that of a lady who'd had too much wine. "Standing there, half-naked. In any rational universe, you'd still have all your clothes on."

He felt a warm flush race over his skin. Perhaps he'd been too quick to remove his shirt—but it had seemed utterly imperative at the time to get himself detached from her. He gestured helplessly at her wrist. "Your *bracelet*—"

She cut him off again, making a sweeping gesture outward with both hands, apparently indicating his height and breadth. "Besides, you're proportioned like a statue of Hercules. No flesh-and-blood man actually *looks* like that."

He was quite sure he was gaping at her again. Why couldn't he keep his jaw shut, like it belonged? "I—I beg your pardon?"

Her forefinger stabbed towards him, as if in accusation. "Nobody actually looks like that," she repeated. "So massive. With all those—those *hard ridges*. Like you're carved out of granite."

"*Granite?*"

"Granite," she affirmed. "So, clearly, I'm imagining you."

He wasn't sure what to answer to that statement. "I'm a soldier," he insisted. "I spend my days in hard physical activity. Many of us look like this. "

"Don't try to hoodwink me," she said, lifting her chin haughtily. "When Christopher was in Parliament, I danced with ballrooms full of officers, and you dwarf the lot of them."

"Oh, *honestly*—"

"And even if all soldiers did look like you, there's still another flaw in your logic."

He stared hard at her, feeling his own head begin to spin. He sighed. "And what would that flaw be?"

"I was married, you know. I saw Christopher take off his coat, night after night."

He wasn't sure where this was going, but he was nearly certain he wasn't going to like it. "No disrespect to your husband, Lady Grantleigh," he said, "but Christopher was not a military man."

"True, but irrelevant to my point. My point has to do with *tailoring*, and the effect of that cannot be very different from man to man, regardless of profession."

"*Tailoring?*"

"Yes. You know—the structure of the garment, the layers of wool, the stiffness and the padding."

"I *know* the definition of tailoring, but—"

She huffed out an impatient breath. "Christopher always looked *smaller* when he took off his coat. That makes perfect sense, like—like an orange looking smaller without its stiff peel. But you don't look smaller without your coat. You look…*bigger*. Quite a bit bigger. It defies the laws of physics." She waved her fingers again, this time in a wide sweep to either side of his neck. "There's no way you fit all those—those *shoulders* inside your coat."

He glanced down at himself, reflexively, as if perhaps his body had swelled without his realizing it. But he looked exactly as he always did.

"It's simply impossible," Julia said. "Ergo, you're an hallucination. And I'll prove it."

Without warning she stepped forward and planted both palms square against the front of his chest, giving him a shove. She hit him rather hard, as though she really hadn't quite expected his bulk to stop her short.

And surprised as he was, all he could think was *her hands are so soft, her hands are so warm.*

"Oh, dear!" she said, blushing horribly, and backing away fast. "Well, you don't *feel* like an hallucination, do you? Rather more like a stone wall." Her retreat only stopped when her calves hit the little leather divan tucked against the far wall. "Oh, I'm sorry, Major Holsworth," she said, sounding quite mortified. "That was—that was ridiculous of me."

In the absence of anything more productive to do, he shrugged. "Given the standard set by the rest of the evening, it was only...*mildly* ridiculous."

That earned a strangled little laugh from her. But then she sank down onto the divan and buried her face in her hands. "Honestly," she said, her voice tight with mortification. "I don't know what's come over me. I really have gone round the bend, haven't I? Flown up in the rafters with the bats and the pigeons?"

"Lady Grantleigh, *please*," he said, taking a step towards her. "I don't know if you're being serious with me right now or not. But, quite frankly, you're—you're worrying the blazes out of me." He wanted to sit down next to her, to try to comfort her, but even he knew that getting so close was something no gentleman should do, not in their current situation.

Julia groaned softly into her palms.

Well, he couldn't just stand here like a useless lump of stone. Of *granite*. He scooped up his shirt from the floor so at least she wouldn't have to be exposed to his...*hard ridges* any longer.

"You must believe me," he said, as he yanked the garment back over his head. "You haven't gone mad. I've seen that happen to men in battle, and—well, it's far worse than anything you're doing. Far, far worse."

She glanced up at him, wiping a fresh spring of tears. "Is that so?"

"That's so. Definitely so."

She nodded, looking perhaps a little relieved. "All right, then. I suppose I'm not actually mad. But I'm certainly not myself. Not at all what I used to be."

He squatted before her, trying to draw in his shoulders, make himself not quite so terrifyingly *massive*. "Well, of course you're not what you used to be," he said. "Naturally, you're not. You're—you're grieving. Your world's been turned on end."

Tears welled again. "Turned inside out," she corrected him, quietly. "Crumpled up, and kicked down a hill. And—and rolled into a ditch."

"Oh," he said. His heart contracted. "That bad?"

She nodded, sniffling again. "That bad." Her shoulders shuddered with another suppressed sob. "And everyone expects me to be cheerful by now, as if *so* much time has passed. They think I should *get on* with life."

A little stab of chagrin went through him. He'd expected that of her, too, hadn't he? Expected her, after a year and half, to have sprung back to the vibrant young woman she'd always been. "I'm so sorry," he said.

"And I thought I was doing better, you know, when I stopped weeping all the time. I get out of bed every day now, and put on a clean frock, plan satisfactory household menus and write letters to my cousins, and from time to time even play the pianoforte."

"Well...that's progress, isn't it?"

"I suppose. But—but it feels like I'm...*drifting*. Like I do it all in a fog."

A painful lump was forming in his throat. "I'm sorry." It felt pathetic, to keep repeating that phrase, but he knew of nothing else to say to her.

Her hands fisted in her skirts, twisting at the cornflower silk. "And Aunt Margaret doesn't seem to understand why I'm still so sad, why I can't adjust to the way things are. To hear her talk about it, her widowhood seems scarcely to have affected her at all."

Ah. "I never met Lord Lambert," he said. "But from what Lady Eleanor's told me, it wasn't much of a love match. Lady Lambert was young, and caught up in romantic illusions, but once the courtship was done, the man showed his true colors as an ill-tempered prig. When he died, she was glad enough to return to her childhood home." He heaved a deep sigh, and couldn't seem to refrain from reaching out and clasping Julia's hands in his own. Thankfully, she didn't pull away. "But *your* marriage," he said. "That was another thing entirely. Christopher was...an extraordinary man, with an extraordinary heart. And he deserves to be mourned deeply. As deeply as can be."

Julia's features crumpled as streams of tears ran down her cheeks. But she was nodding, and he took that as a good sign.

He rubbed his thumbs across the backs of her hands, chafing them gently, like he would with an injured soldier, trying to encourage her. "Anyone with eyes could see how you two loved one another. Christopher lived by your breath. And you—"

"I lived by his." She squeezed Marcus's fingers tight, as if holding on against a tide that was trying to sweep her away. "And now I don't know how I'm supposed to keep breathing."

"But you're doing it already," he insisted. "You *are* breathing. At this very moment. And that's all you need to do— keep on doing it."

"For how long?" she asked, her voice strained. "Until what? He isn't coming back."

"No." *No, he wasn't. Neither of them would ever speak to Christopher again, lay eyes on Christopher again. Ever.*

Sorrow tugged hard at his insides, making his chest sore and heavy.

Even now, it seemed half-unreal to him that Christopher was gone. Weeks had passed before the news reached India, and with the war in progress, Marcus hadn't even been able to accompany Lady Eleanor home for the grand state funeral held the following spring. Some mornings when he woke, his first impulse still was to reach for paper to pen Chris a letter.

"No," Marcus said. "He's not coming back, and that is brutally unfair. That isn't how the universe should work." His throat seemed to close up, and suddenly he had to choke out his words. "I—I miss him, too," he said. "I miss him horribly."

Julia gasped, and, oddly enough, some of the light that had been absent suddenly lit again in her eyes. "Oh, of course you do," she said, her voice soft with compassion. "Here you are, comforting me, and you—well, he was like a brother to you, wasn't he? You've known him—you knew him—forever."

And then, of all things, Julia took her hands from his and placed her palms softly against the sides of his face, one fingertip stroking the scar a Pindari saber had left on his cheek.

Her expression was unguarded, vulnerable, open—not hidden behind her usual formality. The pure brightness of her gaze focused entirely on him, and it sent the sweetest ache through the length of his body.

I would die for her, he thought. *I would gladly die if that would do anything to help her.*

She studied him for a long moment, and he could have sworn she saw straight through skin and bone to the naked center of who he was.

And then she nodded.

"You're *kind*," she said quietly, in a wondering tone, as though it was a revelation to her. "*Kindhearted*, under that fearsome exterior. Christopher always said so. I don't know why I never saw it until now."

A soft, sad smile played on her lips, and all at once he found he, too, wasn't sure how to keep breathing.

Nothing felt quite steady—not his legs, not the floor beneath him, not the walls of the room. The air seemed to have grown warmer, much warmer, as though the boiler in the cellars had been overzealously stoked in the past few minutes. The scent of the orange blossoms in the conservatory seemed to grow thicker around them.

Perhaps he was going a bit mad himself.

Julia's eyes were still scanning his face, her palms warm against his cheeks. The glow of the lamp illumined her like an angel. "It must be awful for you," she said.

Marcus bit at his lower lip. He remembered the corporal bringing him the letter from England, the paper sealed with black wax. He scarcely recalled the actual reading of it, just the sensation of a crushing darkness around him, and a harsh ringing in his ears. He hadn't been able to breathe, then, either.

And he hadn't really spoken to anyone about what he felt. Soldiers didn't do that.

But Julia deserved to know she didn't grieve alone.

"It *was* awful," he said. "When I got the word that he—that he was gone, I could not even comprehend it. It was as if I'd suddenly walked off the edge of the earth."

"Yes!" she said. "Into—into a great void. Black, and—and *terrible*."

He nodded. "I don't even remember the next few days. I suppose I drank a great deal, which is not at all my habit. And then—well, then, there was still a war to fight. I had my duty. A battle to lead. So I pressed on."

"Oh," she said on a sharp breath. "I wish I had some duty. Some *real* duty." Her hands fell back to her lap, balling into fists, and he instantly missed their warm touch. "I'm not even the Countess of Grantleigh anymore, not really. I'm just a placeholder now, until Christopher's cousin Alfred takes a wife."

Her words were bleak, but her tone had no self-pity in it. In fact, even as she spoke, she made a visible effort to straighten her spine. She was trying to pull herself back under control.

But, still, he *felt* her suffering, and it sent a wash of pain through him that nearly dropped him to his knees. What was it like, to be a woman? To have one's whole identity tied up in domestic life? Where a single loss like this could rob one of everything that mattered?

"By any chance," Julia said, "is the army looking for female recruits?"

He chuckled, despite the heaviness in his heart. "No. I'm sorry. Though I suspect you'd make a formidable officer."

That made her laugh as well, a brief, hoarse sound, barely more than a cough. "Formidable? Do you really think so?"

"I have no doubt."

She gave him a wry smile. "I was always the capable one, did you know? Out of all my friends. Sensible, clear-headed, confident Julia. The one to come to for advice. The one who knew what to do, how to behave, how to handle any situation."

"I know that. You have always been most capable. And clear-headed."

"And when I met Christopher, when he chose me, out of all the girls who were vying for his attention, I didn't even realize what a miracle it was. It merely seemed…the next natural step in a life properly lived. I took it for granted. Well, no—I knew I was lucky. But I didn't see how *improbable* it was. How much more I was given than any rational person should expect."

He sighed. "You deserved a love like that. To be loved like that."

She drew herself up even straighter, and her brows arched. "Well, the joke's on me, now, isn't it?" she said, her tone suddenly sharp. "Because Christopher's been taken away. And it turns out I don't know how to live my life. Not at all. Not without him."

Marcus didn't know what to answer to that. He just waited, and listened. Let her say whatever she needed to say.

"You were right, you know," she said. "I *have* grown too thin. I don't eat enough of those meals I plan so diligently." She held up the fingers of her left hand, and flicked her thumb against the base of her ring finger. "Look at my wedding ring. It spins so loose I'm always afraid it will just drop off one day." Her tears brimmed once more, and her breath shuddered. "And then I'll have—nothing. Nothing left of him at all."

And then Marcus couldn't bear it, he just couldn't bear it anymore.

In one swift move, he gathered her in his arms and drew her against him, holding her tight. "Julia," he said, daring to use her name, not her title. "*Julia.*"

And, thank God, she didn't stiffen and pull away, she leaned hard into him, pressing her weight into his chest and burying her face in the crook of his neck. Her arms went around him, too, clutching at the muscles of his back as though she'd sink through the earth without that support. She was gulping for air, her whole body trembling as though it would break apart, and he thought it might kill him if her grief truly did make her run mad.

Desperate to soothe her, he cradled the back of her head in one hand and rubbed her back with the other, whispering soft words, he wasn't even sure what, telling her she wasn't alone, telling her everything would be all right, even though he knew it wouldn't be, knew there was nothing he could do to make any of this better.

Blast it all, he wanted to run his sword through someone, load a cannon and blow something to smithereens. But those skills were useless here.

So he just held her. Held her and whispered whatever comforts came into his head.

Slowly, Julia's trembling stilled. The shuddering stopped, and she gathered herself once more. Finally, she took one hand from his shoulders to draw a handkerchief from the placket of her gown, mopping at her eyes and nose, her lady-like delicacy returning.

When she looked up at him again, her eyes were a bit pink around the edges, but their blue was still piercing. "Thank you," she said, giving him a wobbly smile. "For listening to me. I haven't had anyone to talk to, to *really* talk to, all this time."

He swallowed hard. "You have me," he said, and it felt like he was swearing a vow. "You always have me."

"Oh." Her lips parted on a soft gasp. "I do?"

"Of course. To—to listen to you," he hastened to add. "To listen to whatever you have to say." It took all his force of will not to say more, not to unburden his heart more fully. She wouldn't want to hear all that, surely, all the things he felt about her. It would horrify her.

But his will mustn't have been entirely under his control, because before he knew what he was doing, the hand that had been motionless at the base of her skull slid forward to press against her cheek.

"I am your friend," he told her. "You must know that."

She leaned into his palm, laid her own hand over his knuckles. Her blue eyes locked with his, and the force of her gaze stripped his soul raw. "Yes," she said. "I see that. Christopher always told me you were the best friend anyone could hope to have. And now I understand why."

And then, to his shock, she turned her head towards his hand and pressed a soft kiss into his palm. Just a gentle, chaste touch of her lips, for the slightest instant, but he felt the pulse of it straight through to his belly.

"*Marcus*," she said, trying out his name carefully, and the sound of it on her lips nearly gutted him. "Thank you, Marcus." Her gaze was still so open, still taking him in so completely.

Now his tongue wouldn't quite work. "Of—of course," he managed to say. His arms were still partially around her, one hand pressing the small of her back. She still had one hand resting on his shoulder.

He really ought to let go of her, he really ought to stand up, and retrieve his coat, and button the buttons tight, and put the safe barriers of civilization between them again. But he couldn't seem to draw his hands away.

Some force, some palpable force, seemed to bind the two of them together, and he was powerless to resist it.

He took a deep breath. "You know you may tell me anything," he found himself saying. "And ask me for anything. Anything you need from me, I will give. I swear that to you."

Her eyes went wide at those words, and he could have sworn her pupils darkened, or perhaps grew larger against the brilliant blue. She studied him for a long moment, scanning his features slowly. What on earth was she thinking now?

"Anything?" she asked, her voice soft as breath. "Do you mean that? Do you really mean that?"

"*Anything.*"

And then he was quite sure the madness she had spoken of earlier had suddenly become entirely real, rising up and sweeping over them both.

Because Julia leaned in closer to him, and she slid her arms around his neck once more.

And with a heart-rending sigh, she pressed her mouth to his.

CHAPTER 5

*M*arcus didn't respond at first, his brain frozen as he tried to make sense of what was happening.

Julia was *kissing* him.

It seemed improbable—*impossible*.

And yet, undeniably, he felt the silken softness of her plush lips against his. He felt the soft pressure of her breasts against his chest, the clutch of her fingertips kneading the muscles of his back, and the lavender scent of her hair. Oh, and the subtle heat of her mouth, and the sweet taste of her.

He made a sound in his throat of animal desperation.

Julia pulled back and looked at him uncertainly. Her hands trembled on his shoulders. "Do you—do you want me to stop?"

What he thought was, *Yes. Yes, absolutely.*

Yes, you should stop kissing me, and get the hell out of this room before I drag you into my arms and ravish you, because this is wrong a dozen different ways, and you will regret this, and I will regret this, and once whatever strange impulse has seized you passes, you will hate me forever if I don't stop you now.

But, oh, God, he wanted her. He had always wanted her. And what he saw in her eyes—the need, the profound loneliness, and, great heaven, the raw yearning—it was more than he knew how to fight against.

So somehow what he said was, "No. No, Julia, I don't want you to stop."

Almost without the effort of his will, his hands went to the sides of her head, his fingers spearing through the soft waves of her hair.

His lips came down on hers, and she sighed against them, her breath warm and fragrant, and the surge of wild desire he felt drove out all thoughts of honor or scandal or propriety.

Julia was here, actually in his arms, offering herself, and if he was the one who'd now turned lunatic, he wouldn't have returned to sanity for anything in the world.

Her hands were pulling at the linen of his shirt, trying to draw it upwards. "Take this off again," she murmured against his mouth.

He let go of her just long enough to oblige, stripping the garment off over his head, then pulled her back hard against him, his heart pounding as he felt her arms slide warm and smooth against his bared flesh.

"Better," she whispered, and then her hands were roving over him. Oh, and the feel of them, her eager palms on his shoulders, her chest, his ribs, tracing the shapes of his muscles, sent shock waves through his body. "You're beautiful," she said, in the breaths between kisses. "So beautiful."

"*I'm* beautiful?" Nobody had ever said such a thing about him before.

"Extraordinarily so," she insisted, skimming her hands over his biceps and back up to his shoulders again. "Like something from a dream."

He groaned. His blood roared, and the air in the room seemed to blaze even hotter than before.

She was the beautiful one. So perfectly made, every curve and angle of her. His greedy hands explored her back, the elegant angles of her shoulder blades, the fine tapering of her rib cage, the trim turn of her waist. A lady, every inch of her. She felt tiny and delicate against the breadth of his body, so delicate he feared he might crush her without meaning to if he let the passion rising in him have full rein. But there was a lushness to her as well, where her hips rounded outwards, and in the fullness of her breasts. Her long, slim arms had a strength and solidity greater than he would have expected.

She broke their kiss for just one moment, as one of her hands left his side and reached behind her to the lacings at the back of her gown. "Loosen these," she pleaded. "And my stays. I can scarcely get any air."

Oh, Lord. He tried to keep some grip on his reason, on his sense of what was right. It was one thing for his chest to be bared, but if they started removing her clothing, they'd soon be headed to a point of no return. "Are you sure that's what you want?" he asked.

"To *breathe*?" Her eyes sparkled as they gazed into his, and the effect on him was as heady as brandy. "Yes, don't you remember? You told me yourself it's what I must do."

Damn it all. If there were reasons why he shouldn't let this go forward, he suddenly couldn't remember any of them. Both his hands fell to the base of her spine, and he tugged her lacings loose, whisking the long ties through the eyelets inch by inch upward until her bodice gave way enough for him to drag the silk down from her shoulders. Such lovely shoulders, smooth and white, utterly flawless. The creamy flesh of her breasts swelled deliciously at the top of her stays, and he couldn't stop himself from groaning at the sight.

She might be a lady, but she was also a flesh-and-blood woman.

And very clearly aroused—her lips were swollen and

flushed from his kisses, her eyes alight, her careful coiffure spilling from its pins, and beneath the thin lawn chemise that was the final layer of clothing beneath her stays, the peaks of her breasts visibly hardened to nubs.

As for himself, he was all but shaking with his need for her, the blood driving forcibly downwards through his body, thudding with a deep, primal rhythm, making his cock hard as a length of steel.

Even so, even as he tore at the final set of lacings at the front of her stays, his conscience made one final stand against the force of desire. "Julia," he said, panting. "You should tell me to stop. We will both regret this if we go any farther."

A flicker of hesitation crossed her face, but then she shook her head. "I don't want you to stop," she said, her voice tremulous, but certain. "I *need* you to touch me. Please, Marcus. Touch me. It's been so long since I've been touched."

His fists clenched as he fought down the need that was driving him. "This isn't like you. This isn't the way you've lived your life until now."

She gave a little cry. "Who's to say *what* I'm like, anymore? Who's to say how I should live my life? I can't keep going as I am. You may not be a phantasm, but I'm becoming one. I meant what I said about feeling lost in a fog —everything so cold and numb…"

He squeezed his eyes shut against the assault of contrary feelings within him. "But even if that's what you need, there must be someone else to turn to. Someone better than me. A man who could offer you a proper life—"

"No, Marcus." Her fingers squeezed his shoulders. "I don't want someone else. I don't trust anyone else. It's you— it has to be you. Right now. You swore that you would help me, remember? That you would protect me."

"I don't think Christopher meant it to be like *this*."

"How could he predict what I would need? All I know is

that if you don't touch me now, I'll disappear entirely. I'll dissolve into nothingness. I'll die."

"You won't—"

"Right *now*," she insisted. "I don't care if this is madness. I'm begging you. *Please*."

Please. It was that last word, said with such desperation, that pushed him over the edge.

He wasn't going to think any more. He couldn't think. Seizing her face with both his hands, he crushed his mouth against hers.

It was a claiming kiss, and a pledge.

With a sigh against his lips, she arched her back and pressed in closer against him, the silken softness of her breasts molding still tighter to the hardness of his chest. Her lips parted, yielding to him, and his tongue drove inward, flicking against the soft, slick flesh of her mouth. Desire flared hotter in him, fierce and demanding.

His fingers freed the last loop of the ties of her stays, and he eased the firm shell of it away from her ribs and shoulders, then dropped the whole stiff garment to the floor.

Without that restraint, his hands could move more freely over her body, and he was eager to reach every part of her. Her thin lawn chemise, the final barrier, was gathered along the neckline by a length of silk ribbon. A quick tug to loosen the bow, and that fabric, too, slid loose from her shoulders. Her bosom was bared at last.

He drew back from the kiss so he could look at her, and the heady rush of desire left him dazed. Dear Lord, her breasts were exquisite, lovelier even than he had imagined—firm and high and round, her nipples pink as rosebuds, upturned as if begging for the touch of his tongue.

He was more than happy to oblige.

Ducking his head, he took one pink nub in his mouth, drawing the swell of surrounding flesh deeper with the pull of his lips as his tongue rasped back and forth across the peak.

Julia cried out in pleasure, burying her hands in his hair and drawing his head tighter against her, urging him on. He was happy to oblige that request, too, using lips and teeth and tongue to draw more cries and moans from her, laving one breast and then the other, using his hands to lift the soft mounds from beneath, kneading them gently, and using his fingers to stroke and squeeze whichever nipple was not currently in his mouth.

Her flesh heated beneath his touch, and she arched into him almost violently, demanding more. A harsh impatience drove him, too, as the more primitive parts of his brain began to demand he explore the regions of her body still hidden beneath her silk skirts. His breeches were almost painfully confining now, and to keep from bursting his own buttons he had to take one hand from the delight of her breasts just long enough to release the fall.

His cock sprang forward, thick and hard and urgent as a battering ram, but he ignored its insistent pleas to heave up her skirts immediately and bury it deep within her.

Given the way she was moaning and writhing against his mouth, he suspected Julia would have no objection to hurrying things forward, too. But he intended to take his time with her. She needed to be given pleasure, enormous pleasure, until every last part of her was soft and heated and thrumming with delight—and undeniably alive.

He eased her backward onto the divan now, but with no intent to position himself atop her. He settled her head upon a throw pillow, kissed her once more deeply on the lips, and began to trail hot kisses along the length of her throat and torso. He let himself linger, briefly, on her delicious bare breasts, pausing to draw each one lovingly into his mouth again before moving downward, kissing and stroking her ribs and the taut flesh at the top of her belly. She arched her back and panted as he went, her fingers twisting in his hair and grasping at his shoulders.

Only when the bunched blue silk of her gown around her waist blocked his path downward did he give himself permission to move to the bottom of the divan and grasp the hem of her skirts and begin to push the fabric upwards. So much silk and fine linen—underskirt and petticoats and the lower part of her chemise, so much more than he was accustomed to with the ladies who made their homes in the heat of India. It made him feel like a treasure-seeker.

And the treasure within was worth risking any penalty, any harm, any curse to find.

Her legs were slender, but supple, her calves gracefully curved, gleaming in their fine silk stockings. He slid off her blue silk slippers slowly, carefully, as though he were the royal attendant of a queen, then brushed his fingers inch by inch up the length of her lower leg, kissing as he went, stroking and massaging her flesh, letting her know every inch of her was precious and glorious and worthy of his worship.

Reclining as she was, her hands could not reach him now, and he watched her fingers dig into the leather of the divan, needing to clutch onto something.

Her skirts pooled still between her thighs, preserving some measure of her modesty—the sweet treasure there still hidden, and he schooled himself to patience, giving his attention first to the sensitive place at the backs of her knees, and the soft flesh of the lower part of her thighs where the stockings left one last barrier between her skin and his tongue.

He teased her by licking at her through the silk and blowing soft puffs of air against the moisture. The sensation made her twist beneath him with mewling cries, her fingernails scrabbling against the cushions of the divan.

For the longest time, she made no effort to hurry him, or

to sit up so she could touch him in return. She seemed to understand that he was concerned only with *giving* to her, with letting her feel the beat of warm blood beneath her skin, helping her remember that she was made not of shadow and fog and cold, but of muscle and nerve and living flesh.

At last, though, her patience wore thin. "More, Marcus!" she cried, her voice thick with need. "*Please!*"

He chuckled softly, and moved to oblige her, just as he had with her breasts.

His hands slid upwards, past the top edge of her stockings, and caressed the bare flesh of her upper thighs. And his mouth quickly followed suit, nuzzling and kissing and nipping at the tender curves there until her hands were buried in his hair once more, and the sounds coming from her mouth no longer seemed to come from a civilized being.

And then, and only then, did he push her skirts all the way to her waist, and part her thighs with his hands, and let himself gaze on the most private part of her, at long last bared completely to his view.

He held himself motionless for a long moment, taking in the whole length of her body, her hair spilling wild across the pillow as her writhing worked it free from its pins, her eyes shut tight, her lush mouth open, her lovely breasts glowing in the lamplight, the nipples still taut with need. Her thighs were like a fine carving in alabaster, the dark curls between her legs glistening with her desire.

It was a sight he never in a million years could have thought would be granted him to see. To be here with her like this, after all his years of hopeless yearning, seemed impossible, and yet somehow inevitable, the most natural thing in the world.

And then he could restrain himself no longer. He bent his head between her thighs and put his mouth to the hot, slick core of her.

This tender flesh he lavished with all the passionate attention he had given to her breasts, and more, stroking and laving her, gently parting her folds, teasing the most sensitive nub above them with flicks of his tongue and long, firm circling caresses with the pad of his thumb.

The sweet musky scent of her filled his senses, firing his need, but he did nothing to slake his own desires. He pleasured her on and on, until her thighs trembled and her hips bucked wildly upward, and at last she was clutching at his shoulders, begging him, "Marcus, now, please! I want you, here, with me. Inside me. *Please.*"

This time, he didn't hesitate—he was all too eager to obey her command.

Pushing his breeches lower on his hips, not stopping to try to wrestle off his boots, he stretched himself out above her. She reached up to embrace him, and her eyes were glowing again with brilliant, vital light—a light he would do anything to keep burning there.

"You're alive, Julia," he told her, low and urgent, "Very much alive."

"*Alive,*" she answered fervently, and she wrapped one of her arms around his waist, drawing his hips down to the cradle of her thighs.

A rush of tenderness went through him, mixed with wonderment and desperate, ravaging need. He would have stayed there forever, just drinking in the sight of her face, but his blood was turning quickly to fire. The head of his cock already jutted against the hot, wet entry of her cleft, and it throbbed with urgency to thrust inside her.

She seemed more than ready.

He used one hand to guide the head gently between her silken folds, groaning at the sweet feel of her.

She moaned in answer. "*Please,*" she pleaded again. "All of you. Everything, please."

He was the one trembling now, fighting the urge to pound hard inside of her. Her husband had been a far smaller man, far more civilized by his very nature, and Marcus didn't want to hurt her or terrify her with his size or with his passion.

And he was wise to be cautious with her. Slick and ready as she seemed to be, he'd slid only a few inches into her before her sheath clenched too tight to admit him easily farther.

"Oh," she said, gasping, "there's—there's a great deal of you."

He reared back on his elbows. "Am I hurting you?"

"Yes, a little," she admitted, and bit at her lower lip. "No…I don't know." Her head writhed again on the pillow.

"It's all right," he whispered, keeping his weight on his elbows, kissing her gently along her temple, along the line of her jaw, giving her time to adjust to his breadth. "We don't have to rush anything."

"No—don't stop," she said, her blue eyes locking on his. "Keep going."

He thrust a bit harder, and, *sweet heaven*, the tight, tight clench of her around the head of his cock was almost too much to bear. He was like a cannon primed and loaded, where one small spark could be enough to set his fuse blazing.

Beneath him, she was panting, gasping, her legs and arms tensed, her fingers biting into his back.

He pressed his kisses along her throat, up against her ear. "Relax, Julia," he urged her. "Just relax. Relax and trust me." He slid one hand beneath the curve of her bottom, tilting her hips upward to let him angle into her more gently, then used the other to stroke her again at that sensitive peak just above where they were joined.

He stroked and kissed and whispered, and a little at a

time, her inner muscles eased. Then all at once, her passage gave up its fierce resistance, and he slid deep.

"Oh!" she cried.

He froze. "Am I still hurting you?" he gasped. "Did that hurt?"

"No," she answered on a moan. "That's good—that's so good."

"Thank God!" He didn't know if he could have stopped himself from thrusting now no matter what she said.

He pushed himself into her to the hilt, into the deep, hot core of her, and it stunned him to think he was *inside* of her, fully inside, after all these years of wanting. He let himself relish that sensation for a moment, the perfect tightness as her sheath gripped him, before he pulled himself backward, partway out of her again.

And then he rocked forward, feeling her flesh part for him, caress him, embrace him fully. He went in harder, and out, surfacing and diving deep over and over, everything in his universe focusing on those sensations, the slide, the heat, the slippery clench of her muscles inside, the intimate, utter contact between these most private parts of themselves.

She gave herself without hesitation, trembling beneath him, moaning, her nails raking his back, and her passionate response made him burn all the more.

He pumped into her, into her heat and tightness and wetness, and soon bursts of lightning seemed to race outward from his hips, all along his spine. The main force of it gathered heavily in his belly and in the small of his back. His shoulders strained, his cock grew harder and longer, seeming ready to burst.

Her legs clamped around him, her calves urging him on, and he could feel her sheath tightening once more, in the best possible way this time.

She was crying out, close to reaching her peak, and as his

hips rocked against her, he made sure she felt the pressure where she needed it, at that place where he'd made her moan earlier with his touch. His back arched now, as the sensations shook him.

It wasn't going to take either one of them much longer.

"Marcus," she cried, seeking out his mouth with hers, and thrusting her tongue past his lips to tangle with his.

He drew her tongue deeper, scraping it lightly with his teeth, suckling it, admitting her into him as she had let him so deep inside her.

His hips rocked against hers, again and again, harder and harder, finding a rhythm that seemed to come from somewhere beyond them, where he could scarcely tell who moved, who gave and who took. He was lost to himself, lost in her.

It seemed they might go on forever that way, the barriers between them melting, rippling together into one flesh, one energy. But then at last Julia's head fell back, her hands convulsing against his shoulders, her thighs shuddering, and she cried out in ecstasy as her sheath gripped and pulsed almost violently around him.

"Julia," he gasped as he felt her give herself over to him so completely, so unreservedly. But what he was thinking was *I'm home, I'm home, I'm home.*

He held back from his own final pleasure until her spasms slowed, but then he was at the moment of crisis himself, irreversibly, and desperately as he wanted to pour himself deep into her, he found the discipline somehow at the last moment to pull out from her, snatch up his fallen shirt from the floor, and spend his seed hard into the cloth.

And then he could do nothing but fall atop her, utterly spent, and let her bury her face against his throat. She was breathing hard, still, and he thought perhaps he felt the wetness of tears against his neck.

Her held her tight as whatever emotions working

through her found their release, stroking her hair back from her temple with one hand.

He had no words to say. He couldn't stop his head from spinning, much less decide what on earth they were supposed to do when they came back to their senses again.

It was enough now—it would have to be enough—just to hold her, and breathe with her, and drink in the scent of her hair. Just let himself sink into the wonder of having her in his arms, having her pressed up so tight and warm against him, still clinging to him as though she wanted him as desperately as he wanted her.

That was an illusion, surely, but it was the sweetest illusion he had ever known.

He could allow himself to indulge it just a little longer.

But, of course, the universe would never be so kind to him. Just as Julia seemed to be calming again, her breathing slowing to a more natural rhythm, her grip on his back becoming gentle rather than tense, he heard hurried footsteps outside in the conservatory.

And Lady Lambert's worried voice.

"Julia!" she was calling. "Julia, dear, where on earth have you gone? Are you hiding here somewhere?"

A jolt of adrenaline went through him, and Julia stiffened in his arms and quietly gasped, "Aunt Margaret!"

He laid a finger across her lips. "The door is locked," he breathed against her ear. "Even if she tries it, she'll assume some other couple has snuck off to avail themselves of the privacy of this room. She won't think it's you."

"Couples don't behave like that in Devonshire!" Julia whispered back.

He gave an ironic glance down at their half-naked, entwined bodies. "In fact, I believe they do," he said. "It's quite the scandalous place." And he had to stifle a laugh at the look of shock on her face.

Well, better to laugh about their situation than to weep.

They waited, then, nearly holding their breath, until Lady Lambert's footsteps retreated back in the direction of the ballroom.

When it was clear they were truly alone again, Julia looked him in the eye, squaring her jaw stubbornly. "Well, I'm not sorry," she said fiercely.

"And you have no need to be," he assured her. *But in the morning, you may feel differently*, he thought, and felt a knot form heavily in his gut.

There was nothing for it then but to rise and dress as quickly as they could manage, before Lady Lambert thought Julia had truly come to grief, and raised a general hue and cry. The last thing Julia's reputation needed was all her friends and neighbors crowding into the hothouse room to find her *en déshabillé* with a lower-class lover.

That truly wasn't the way Julia behaved, at least not in her life until this point.

And somehow he couldn't imagine her making a habit of it.

He'd been there to serve—to *protect* her, as she put it—in a time of desperation, that was all. And now it was done. And he had no right to expect anything more.

She'd given him her body tonight, because she needed some physical demonstration of her survival—the human, flesh-and-blood part of her had needed that. But she'd been very clear about her heart. That could never be his. Her heart still belonged to Christopher Grantleigh, whose lady she would forever be.

So he helped lace her back into her gown, found her slippers, made his uniform as presentable as he could manage. "You make your way back up to your room by whatever private means you can," he told her. "I'll find Lady Lambert and tell her I found you seeking a breath of air out in the gardens, and that I sent you back inside. She can send a maid up to check on you."

Julia nodded absently, her cheeks still flushed, as she pushed a few pins haphazardly back into the tumbled chaos of her hair. Her eyes had a slightly wild look.

"Are you all right, Julia?" he asked her. "You—you don't really think you've—"

"Gone mad?" she finished for him. "No. Not mad. Perhaps I've lost my head in other ways tonight." She flashed him a small, tight smile. "But I'm sane enough."

She looked down at her rumpled skirts, licking at her lips, clearly at a loss for what else she ought to say or do. The inevitable regret, he feared, was already beginning to take hold of her.

He longed to brush his hand across her cheek, to kiss her one last time.

He wanted to make her promise she would speak to him again on the morrow, not hate him forever for what they'd just done. But touching her, kissing her, asking her for promises—those things seemed as forbidden to him now as they had been on the day they'd first met, the day he'd fallen irrevocably in love with her.

Maybe even more so, somehow.

So, as she hovered in the doorway, he sketched her a formal bow and bid her good night, giving her the easiest excuse he could to turn and hurry out the door.

And he watched in an old, familiar, quiet agony as she slipped out of the room, and out of his arms forever.

CHAPTER 6

The next morning, Julia woke with a start.

Though she was in her own familiar bed, it took a moment to make sense of her surroundings. She was alone, and for the first time in many months, that fact surprised her.

Her thighs ached, her cheeks stung from the scrape of beard stubble, her breasts felt a tenderness almost like bruising. And her pulse still thrummed in her veins.

She was most certainly not numb, not a phantom. Her body felt more real and solid than it had in months. Perhaps ever. *Lord*, Christopher had made love to her a thousand times during their marriage, but she'd never felt the aftermath so clearly the next morning.

Christopher.

The thought of him made the breath catch in her throat.

What would Christopher think if he knew what she and Holsworth—what she and *Marcus*—had done last night?

Would Christopher forgive her?

Would he condemn her?

Would he *understand*?

Her chest felt strange and heavy as she rang for her maid Peggy, and picked up the rosewood hairbrush Christopher had given her, to begin to work the unaccustomed tangles from her hair.

Thankfully, when Peggy arrived, the little maid chattered cheerfully as ever as she helped Julia bathe and fastened her into a new muslin frock—a soft shade of yellow, Aunt Margaret would be pleased to see, not black. She seemed blissfully unaware of her mistress's shocking behavior the night before.

The sun was shining outdoors, the other servants could be heard bustling about the other chambers just as usual. No sulfurous stink of retributive divine thunderbolts emanated from the conservatory.

In the light of day, it seemed almost impossible last night had even happened.

But it *had* happened. Flashes of the memory pulsed through Julia's mind, making her shiver, making her jolt— her body stretched out beneath Marcus's, her palms gripping his enormous shoulders, his great glorious weight pressing her down into the leather of the divan, his hands stroking her everywhere, and her mouth and his…

"My lady?" asked her maid, letting go of the sleeve she'd been fastening. "Did I stick you with a pin?"

"What?" asked Julia, startled.

"You gasped, ma'am. Did I hurt you?"

"No," she said hastily, trying to smile. "No, of course not, Peggy. I just—it's just that I feel so odd wearing colors again."

The lie made her throat heat. She had no business just now playing the loyal widow. She'd debauched herself quite thoroughly last night under her husband's roof, with a man her husband had considered as close as a brother. And, as clear as her reasons had seemed to her in the moment, she couldn't quite recall them now. Just that, at the time, she'd felt she must either use her body, or go cold forever.

She scarcely knew how to *name* what had happened. Lovemaking with Christopher had always been joyous, so full of sweetness. But last night—that was something else, something more primal, more vigorous, more desperate than what she'd known in the marriage bed. Her muscles trembled even now as she remembered the sheer force of the sensations that had swept through her.

What kind of woman was she to have responded as she did?

And where had that side of Holsworth come from?

Peggy tugged her sleeve to rights again. "Oh, but you mustn't feel odd, ma'am," the maid said breezily. "His lordship would be so pleased to see you like this. He always said how pretty you looked in yellow."

Julia's heart gave a painful twist. "Thank you, Peggy," she managed to say. Lord knows, Christopher *did* always say she looked pretty in yellow. He said she looked pretty in any color. He'd been as adoring of her in the sixth year of their marriage as he'd been on their wedding night.

Oh, *Christopher.*

Of course, she'd always adored him, truly, in return. She loved him still, and always would. What happened last night didn't change that, couldn't detract from it.

She did not love Marcus Holsworth. She knew she didn't.

Marcus, she thought again, despite her better judgment, the unfamiliar name taking on a new shape and solidity, sending strange tendrils of feeling through her chest.

What was she supposed to think about him? He really had been so…*different* last night. Passionate, yes. But also kind, and gentle, and full of understanding. Solid as a rock for her, keeping her from sliding over the edge of a dangerous despair.

And she couldn't deny that, in his arms, for a few moments at least, she'd felt part of him, merged with him, as he'd made her icy loneliness melt in the heat of pleasure and desire.

It was all so damnably confusing.

The inside of her nose began to tingle, along with the pressure of impending tears.

But, *no*. She wasn't a child, and she wasn't going to cry. Certainly, she'd bring no honor to Christopher's memory if she gave in to hysterics and made last night's mad, impulsive act a matter of public knowledge.

She squared her shoulders as Peggy finished with her laces and tied a bow in the spring-green ribbon around her waist. Julia had never been the sort to wallow in regret. If regret was even what she felt about what happened in the hothouse room. She honestly didn't know.

Holsworth, she reminded herself. That was his name, not Marcus. She needed to think of him only as Holsworth again, as her husband's gruff, unapproachable, cold-minded friend.

That was all he was ever meant to be to her. All he could ever reasonably be.

Instinctively, her right hand closed around the bracelet that still hung on her left wrist. She sought out the little pin with her fingertip, pressed down as she had when she finally fell into her bed last night, but the clasp held as stubbornly fast as ever.

What if she had never slipped it on in the first place?

None of this would have happened. Even if she and Holsworth had collided in the conservatory, they'd simply have apologized to one another and gone back to the ball-room. Danced one civil dance for Aunt Margaret's sake and then ignored one another, just as she'd originally intended.

And I'd still be floating in that cold, gray, numbing fog ...

She heaved a deep, bracing breath. Well, there was nothing to do for it this morning but to put one foot in front of the other and proceed with her life. *Keep breathing*, that was what he'd said.

In all likelihood, Holsworth had done the reasonable thing by now and hurried back to London. That was how gentlemen handled themselves after indiscretions with worldly widows, so she understood from the gossip of her friends. Well, Holsworth might not truly be a gentleman, but he was certainly a man of the world who understood such matters. And she was no green girl who would need apologies, or coddling, or hasty, reckless vows.

Perhaps he'd head right back to India, even. Perhaps they'd never see one another again.

Her stomach plummeted a little at the thought.

But as she took the stairs down to the breakfast room, she felt almost steady again. If only she'd been able to take the bracelet off, she'd have felt quite in command of herself—but the gold circlet skimmed against the bannister with a light humming noise, like a whispering voice, reminding her how it had pinned her wrist to Holsworth's chest, how her fingers had brushed his jaw. How her arms had wrapped around his back, and clung to him so hard.

Oh, its gleam in the morning sunlight recalled its shimmer in the lamp-light as she buried her hands in Holsworth's hair while he thrust inside her. Reminded her how, even when she'd squeezed shut her eyes at the end, the stunning pleasure that tore through her had seemed like waves of light rippling, a sunburst of the very same golden brightness as the bracelet itself.

She had to stop on the stairs now, close her eyes, grip the bracelet tight with her free hand again as though that would be enough to shut out the remembered sensations. It felt warm beneath her palm. Her blood, too, began to heat and hum, and she almost thought she caught the scent of Holsworth's body in the air. *Marcus's body.*

Dear heaven.

She really needed to get herself back under control.

Her thumb jabbed once more against the bracelet's tiny gold pin. The clasp had better open soon, or she'd have to send one of the footmen to fetch a saw.

There. That thought brought her self-possession back.

She took hold of the bannister again, straightened her spine, and descended the rest of the way like a queen.

But the moment she opened the breakfast room door, she saw how wrong she'd been to assume Holsworth would behave as most Society gentlemen would do: he was sitting right there at the Grantleigh breakfast table, next to Aunt Margaret, the two of them chatting over a spread newspaper.

Julia's heart nearly stopped. A sound forced its way out of her mouth that was somewhere between a sob and a squeak. The strength drained from her legs, and for a moment, she thought she might actually pitch forward onto the carpet.

As Holsworth noticed her in the doorway, gripping the doorjamb for support, he flinched, but he turned the action adroitly into rising to his feet to acknowledge her. His eyes flashed a meaningful look—an apology, perhaps? An unspoken plea to act as though everything were normal?

Aunt Margaret seemed oblivious to the tension in the air, smiling at Julia and beckoning her to take the closest chair. "Julia, darling," she said, in her usual good-natured way. "Can you believe Major Holsworth arranged a room for last night at the Boar's Head Inn? He tried to go there after the dancing ended, but of course I forbade it, and sent his valet to retrieve his luggage." She laid her age-spotted hand on top of Holsworth's, patting it as though he were still a small boy. "Grantleigh Hall is his proper home, after all, and he shall sleep in his own bed so long as he is in Devonshire."

Sweet heaven. Of course Aunt Margaret felt that way.

And of course Holsworth couldn't refuse if she pressed him to stay. He could hardly tell Christopher's elderly auntie he couldn't spend the night at Grantleigh Hall because he'd just enjoyed extensive Biblical knowledge of her niece-by-marriage in the hothouse room.

So, as she crossed the breakfast room, Julia managed a smile of her own. "You were quite right to do so, Aunt," she said. "Christopher surely would have had it no other way." The words caught in her throat, wedged down by a sudden knot of guilt.

Holsworth looked up at her again for a moment, and this time she was quite sure she saw anguish in his eyes. At least he recognized the extreme awkwardness of their position.

But—oh, Lord—there was a part of her that wanted, even now, to pull him with her back to that secret little room, and resume the very…*position* they'd been in on the divan.

Her cheeks burned.

What sort of wanton had she suddenly turned into?

Holsworth cleared his throat abruptly. "May I fix a plate for you, Lady Grantleigh? The—the bacon is quite excellent."

"Yes, thank you," she answered as she hurriedly took a seat beside Aunt Margaret. *Anything to have you move to the other side of the room for a moment, so I won't catch the scent of your cologne again. Or start remembering being held against the extraordinary breadth of your chest.*

It didn't matter what foods he chose for her. Her appetite had quite disappeared, anyway.

As Holsworth went to the buffet, Aunt Margaret leaned in conspiratorially, clasping Julia by the elbow. "Dear Marcus was keeping secrets from us last night," she whispered, though loud enough that the major could no doubt hear her clearly.

Julia's shoulders stiffened. "Secrets?"

"Wonderful secrets!" Aunt Margaret exclaimed, even louder now, her voice vibrating with happiness. "And so unexpected! Such a naughty boy not to tell us directly!"

Naughty boy? Oh, he knew how to be naughty, that was for certain. But surely that wasn't what Aunt Margaret was referring to.

The old lady clapped her hands together, and joyously exclaimed, "Oh, now that I know, I can't hold my tongue! Can you imagine, Julia? There's been a wedding!"

The blood drained from Julia's face. A *wedding*?

Good God—was Holsworth *married*?

Had she done what she'd done last night with a *married man*?

A wave of nausea swept through her. She might be able to forgive herself for losing control last night, but not if the man she was with was sworn to another living woman.

Would Holsworth *do* that? Betray his vows to a lady to whom he was *wed*? Was he really, after all, so uncivilized?

Holsworth's body had gone very still, the plate of food he'd been filling suspended in midair.

"Major Holsworth," Julia managed to say, her voice trembling only slightly. "Can it be that I owe you congratulations?"

"Holsworth?" exclaimed Aunt Margaret. "No, dear, not him. It's far more startling than that!" She turned her head to the foyer, where footsteps were approaching. "Oh, I believe you are about to see for yourself!"

Before the sensation of relief had time to sweep its way through Julia's body, the breakfast room door opened, and a stout, gray-haired woman stepped in.

In looks, she was virtually the double of Aunt Margaret, though slightly older, and wearing a voluminous sash of gold-embroidered sheer red silk over her white dress, draped across one shoulder and gathered about her hips in the Indian style.

Great heavens—with everything that had happened afterward, Julia had forgotten the news Holsworth told her last night. "Aunt Eleanor," she cried, leaping to her feet and hurrying forward, throwing her arms out for an embrace. "Aunt Eleanor! It *is* you!"

With a warm laugh, the older woman wrapped Julia in a tight hug, and kissed her soundly on both cheeks. The good familiar scent of the gardenia powder both sisters habitually dusted over their shoulders filled Julia's nose.

"Let me get a look at you!" Aunt Eleanor said, and drew back slightly to begin her scrutiny. "Oh, my! You're lovelier than ever! I was so worried when I was home for the state funeral—you looked pale enough then to be at death's door yourself. But now! I don't know what Margaret was complaining of in her letters—you have roses galore in your cheeks!"

Julia felt herself blush all the more deeply at that. She didn't really want to consider what exactly had put those roses there.

"It was the ball last night!" interjected Aunt Margaret. "I told you, Julia, that giving up your widow's weeds and joining society again would do you a world of good."

Now Eleanor's blue eyes sparkled with rising tears, though the smile didn't leave her face. "That's just as Christopher would want it, you know. His Julia healthy and happy again, and embracing whatever life has in store for her."

*Embracing . . .*oh, good Lord. Did she really have to choose that exact word, just now?

Julia couldn't help glancing over at Holsworth. He was turned toward Eleanor, a look of composed politeness on his face. The plate of food he held, though, was tipping at a rather alarming angle, with a mound of coddled eggs about to slide over onto the floor.

"Oh, Marcus!" cried Eleanor, noticing the impending disaster as well. "Be careful, dearest! You're about to lose your breakfast!"

He blinked down at the plate in sudden awareness, and hurriedly reached right over the table to deposit it between Julia's knife and fork. "It's Lady Grantleigh's breakfast, actually," he said, too hastily to be convincingly cavalier about the matter.

Dash it all. His nerves were as plain as the nose on his face. Eleanor was a notoriously clever woman, and it wouldn't do to give her clues that the relationship between Christopher's widow and Christopher's best friend involved anything a gentleman ought to be nervous about.

But Eleanor only beamed at the major just as adoringly as Margaret tended to do. "Well, that's perfect! There's no one better, Julia, to take care of you than our wonderful Marcus," she said. "He's the very most capable of men." She grinned impishly. "This morning's plate handling excepted, perhaps."

"Beg pardon, Lady Eleanor," he answered, with a slight bow. "I was distracted, as always, by your beauty."

Eleanor and Margaret erupted in identical hooting bursts of laughter. "Oh, yes!" said Eleanor, gripping Holsworth affectionately by the elbow. "And he's good for turning a woman's head with compliments, as well!"

Turning a woman's head. Yes, he was certainly good at that. And he had considerable talents with a woman's other body parts as well.

Oh, dear. The topic of conversation really needed to change.

And then she remembered—*a wedding.*

If it wasn't Marcus who had gotten married, then…

85

Before Julia could ask the question, another set of footsteps echoed in the foyer hallway. And she was quite startled to see the man who entered—a man of about Eleanor's age, dressed in the tailored clothes of an English gentleman, but clearly not of English origin himself.

He was little taller than Eleanor, with a similar shade of silver hair, but his skin was a rich copper-brown shade, and his eyes, behind a pair of gold-rimmed glasses, were the deepest black.

"Julia, dear," said Aunt Eleanor, wrapping an arm around Julia's waist. "Allow me to present Mr. Kalyan Maji, my husband." She extended her other hand to the gentleman who had just entered, and linked her fingers with his. "*Meri jaan*," she said to him, "this is Lady Grantleigh, the wife—the widow—of my dearest nephew, Christopher."

Good gracious. The man was Indian.

Well, Eleanor had never lived her life by the rules other English gentlewomen considered themselves bound by. She'd refused to marry at all, for one thing, for so many years. But now, apparently, she'd chosen to make a marriage that would cause most English nobles to shun her completely.

For a moment, Julia was too surprised to do anything but stare.

The gentleman stepped forward, giving Julia a tentative smile. His eyes were kindly, but had same sort of piercing intelligence Eleanor's always had. "It's quite all right to be unsure what to do about me," he said, in a low voice with a rich, musical lilt. "I believe you English would say a marriage such as this is *not at all the thing*. You can understand why, when we realized the household was entertaining the neighbors last night, we chose to enter quietly, and wait to reveal ourselves until the family was alone."

"Oh," said Julia, feeling herself begin to blush. "Well, I —" So much for knowing what to say on any occasion—

none of her careful social training was of any use at all just now.

"Don't worry," said Eleanor, giving Julia a squeeze. "If it makes you feel any better, when I was first presented to Mr. Maji's mother and grandmother, they were so horrified he hadn't chosen a proper Hindu bride, they vowed to starve themselves until he changed his mind about marrying me."

Mr. Maji grinned ruefully. "That vow lasted less than a fortnight. Last I saw them, they were stuffing themselves happily enough with a platter of lamb curry and figs, and seemed satisfied with merely ignoring my presence in the room. Until they needed me to pass the sugar bowl, at any rate—and then they were careful to be extremely rude about it."

Oh, dear. And now *she* was being terribly rude. "Forgive me," Julia said. "You caught me by surprise, that's all. Of course, Mr. Maji, you are very welcome to Grantleigh Hall. Congratulations on your marriage." She scrambled through her memories for the word Christopher had taught her, the lovely greeting that was meant to honor the spirit of the person one was speaking to. *Ah, yes*, she remembered. "Namaste."

Mr. Maji smiled again, with a look of great warmth this time. He pressed his palms together at the center of his chest and bowed. "Namaste," he said.

"There," said Eleanor with satisfaction, patting Julia's back. "I knew you would prove more open-hearted than the typical British lady. As for those who won't accept us, either here or in India, neither my husband nor I care a whit for Society. You know I've a lifetime's experience ignoring the world's opinion. And Mr. Maji and I are quite content in our lovely Calcutta bungalow, with a garden full of jasmine and the freedom of our library."

"Well," said Margaret, coming up beside her sister. "I say it is simply wonderful. Imagine finding love at Eleanor's age!"

"What has age to do with it?" asked Mr. Maji graciously, bowing now towards his wife. "A lady like my wife is young as springtime, always."

Christopher's aunts both laughed again, delightedly.

"Goodness, Mr. Maji," said Margaret. "You'll give Major Holsworth a run for his money in the compliments department. That was wonderfully poetic!"

Holsworth had been standing off to the side quietly while the introductions were being made, but he came forward now, inclining his head towards Eleanor's new husband. "You should know, Lady Lambert, Lady Grantleigh," he said, "that Mr. Maji is a much-renowned scholar of classical Indian poetry. From a great family of renowned scholars."

"Oh!" said Margaret. "Then no wonder you've made a match with my sister, Mr. Maji. She has always been a devoted student of literature and languages. As Christopher was."

"Your sister is a superb scholar," said Mr. Maji, beaming at his wife. "In fact, we met while working in my aunt's literary archives."

"His aunt has the second finest library in all of West Bengal," said Eleanor. "And that is saying a great deal, if you know the literary treasures of that area. She's a far more free-thinking lady than Mr. Maji's mother and grandmother turned out to be, and the moment she learned I was a student of Indian languages, she graciously gave me permission to work on some translations there."

"Oh, goodness!" said Julia suddenly, remembering what a gracious lady should be doing, at least in England. "How rude of me to leave everyone standing here so long. Have you had a chance to eat breakfast, Mr. Maji?" She glanced at the sideboard, wondering if the English fare would be at all to his liking, and gestured with her left hand towards the kitchens. "If there's something else you would like, I can send to Cook for—"

Before she could finish the phrase, both Aunt Eleanor and Mr. Maji made loud gasps of astonishment.

Aunt Eleanor was pointing at Julia's wrist, her eyes wide. "That bracelet!" she cried, "That's *my* bracelet! How on earth did it get *here*?"

Julia glanced down at the gold circlet on her wrist. In all the excitement about Eleanor's marriage, she'd forgotten it was there at all.

"Oh!" she said, feeling a prickling unease down the back of her neck. "But—but weren't you were the one who put it in my chambers last night?"

"No!" said Eleanor, her gaze quite fixed on the bracelet, her head shaking slowly side to side. "No, I most certainly was not. In fact, I couldn't have. I lost it before we left for our journey here. More than three months ago, during our honeymoon in Mumbai. I looked everywhere for it before we returned to Calcutta, and I was sure I'd never see it again!"

Mr. Maji looked just as dumbfounded, but he gave a little shrug. "Perhaps when you first lost it, it became entangled with some garment or other. One of your maids might have packed the garment away with our things in Mumbai without even realizing the bracelet was there. It could easily have slipped into one of those little silk pockets inside your valise, and remained hidden until we arrived here."

Eleanor gave him a dubious look. "Perhaps so. But even if all that were true, how did it get *out* of the valise? Did it jump out, and roll its way into Julia's bedchamber?"

Her husband shrugged again. "Perhaps it tumbled out when one of the Grantleigh maids unpacked for us last night. Its clasp may have caught in *her* skirts, after which she walked with it into Lady Grantleigh's rooms without being aware of its presence, and it came loose again there."

"That's a great deal of subterfuge for a bracelet," said Eleanor, wrinkling her brow.

Mr. Maji smiled, and his eyes twinkled. "But we both know it is a rather remarkable bracelet."

Unexpectedly, a slight blush stained Aunt Eleanor's cheeks. "Indeed, it is."

Julia shook her head at the two of them. "But it *couldn't* have tangled in anyone's skirts," she blurted out. "It was in a box when I found it."

Eleanor and Mr. Maji exchanged newly astonished glances. "A box?" they said at the same time.

"Yes," she said. "A little carved sandalwood box—"

Eleanor's mouth gaped. "With a dancing woman on the lid?"

"Yes!"

"Ha!" said Eleanor, giving her husband a pointed look. "Explain that, *meri jaan*. How on earth did it get back inside its box? I most certainly didn't put it there. I did keep the box with the rest of my jewelry, but you know I never took the bracelet off. Not intentionally, anyway." And suddenly she blushed again, quite deeply this time.

The color in Mr. Maji's cheeks deepened as well, and he cast his gaze downward, a little smile playing on his lips. "I know quite well that you did not," he said.

Holsworth stepped forward now, looking suddenly rather thunderous. "Will someone please explain what is going on here?"

"I cannot," said Mr. Maji. "At least I cannot explain how the bracelet came to be in Lady Grantleigh's chamber. That is most mysterious."

Oh, great heavens. Julia wanted no more talk of mysteries, or the older couple's reasons for blushing. The bracelet had unsettled her own world quite enough already, and she couldn't bear to feel her grip on reason wobble again, as it had last night.

"Well, never mind how it got into my room," she said, hastening to try the clasp again. "If the bracelet's yours, Aunt Eleanor, I shall happily return it." She fumbled again for the tiny gold pin, but pressing it did no more good now than it had the last dozen times she'd tried. "It's just—I'm afraid the catch seems not to be working just now."

Mr. Maji's eyebrows climbed. "No?"

"I don't know what's wrong with it," said Julia. "It worked easily enough the first time I tried it, but now it just won't budge."

Eleanor cast another sideways glance at her husband, her own eyes gleaming now. "Yes, well…it's been known to be a bit tricky."

"Indeed," he answered, seeming to suppress an amused grin. "The bracelet is very old, I believe. And perhaps not entirely in tune with the spirit of modern conveniences."

Reflexively, Julia glanced over at Holsworth, but he seemed as puzzled by the conversation as anyone, and was scowling at the bracelet as though it were a new recruit who wouldn't stop marching out of step.

"Ah, well," said Mr. Maji. "In some matters, logic cannot be our guide." He glanced over at Holsworth now himself, a look of speculation on his face. "But perhaps we should do as Lady Grantleigh suggested, and go somewhere we can sit down. And perhaps more comfortably than we can in this room. I broke my fast early this morning, and need no more. But there is a story behind that bracelet that I think it really would be best for you to hear."

CHAPTER 7

*M*argaret, at least, seemed eager to hear Mr. Maji's story, for she shooed everyone quickly over into the parlor, and ushered each one to comfortable chairs. Unfortunately, she was quite insistent about seating Major Holsworth on the divan next to where Julia had seated herself.

It was hard enough keeping a grip on her composure here in front of Christopher's family when they were simply in the same room. Sharing the same piece of furniture was a challenge she didn't know if she was up for until she made some more sense of her feelings.

She edged carefully towards the far side of the cushion, up against the padded chintz arm. But Holsworth was so large, it was difficult to put much space between them. Though she turned all her attention toward Mr. Maji, who had made himself at home in an armchair beside the fireplace, she could *feel* Holsworth there, warming the air beside her.

Mr. Maji, meanwhile, crossed one leg comfortably over the other knee, and leaned back, looking out over his audience in the manner of an experienced storyteller who knew he had an enthralling tale to tell.

"You should know, Lady Grantleigh," Mr. Maji began, "that according to stories passed down in my family, the bracelet currently adorning your arm fits the description of one said to belong to a very distant relative of mine—an aunt, you might say, but many generations back."

"Many generations?" Forgetting Holsworth for the moment, Julia raised her arm to catch the morning sunlight. Could the bracelet really be so old? The gold still looked so bright and flawless, with no signs of the dents or scratches long use would almost surely bring.

"We have no concrete records to prove this aunt even existed," said Mr. Maji, "but the stories say her name was Bharati. They say she was a scholar, like so many in our line, and made great study of the Gaha Sattasai of the Satavahana King Hala."

"The *what*?" asked Aunt Margaret.

"A great collection of Prakrit poems," said Mr. Maji. And then he leaned forward with a conspiratorial smile. "*Love* poems."

"And *such* poems!" declared Aunt Eleanor, who had claimed the armchair across from her husband, on Holsworth's side of the divan. "Each verse very short, but so full of passion—about illicit love, heartbreak, star-crossed lovers finding the briefest bliss in secret trysting places. Extraordinarily lovely, and so often sad."

Illicit love. Trysting places. Good Lord. Julia was not going to look in Holsworth's direction. She was *not*. Yet somehow she felt the heat and solidity of him even more than she had a few moments before.

She turned her gaze deliberately to the portrait above the hearth, the fifth Earl Grantleigh on horseback, cantering along with his foxhounds bounding beside him. His expression as he looked down over the parlor had always seemed benevolent, but this morning his painted face seemed to glare at Julia in disapproval. She lowered her eyes hastily to the carpet.

"Bharati, it is said," Mr. Maji continued, "lived out one such story of heartbreak in her own life. She fell in love with a young man whom her father would not permit her to marry—no one remembers the reason why not. But she defied her family to be with him."

Aunt Eleanor broke in again, her expression aglow with deep feeling. "Bharati and her lover found happiness, extraordinary happiness," she said. "But only for a very short time. Bharati's family considered her dalliance with this man to be an intolerable dishonor. So, one morning, her brothers used some subterfuge to lure her beloved out into the forest, and then shot him full of arrows."

"Oh, no!" cried Margaret, who had been listening wide-eyed and enraptured. "They killed him, only because he loved the girl! It's like the tragedy of Romeo and Juliet!"

Mr. Maji nodded. "It *was* a great tragedy for Bharati. She never recovered from the loss. But if our family stories are true, she turned her heartbreak into a wonderful book of poetry, in the style of traditional Prakrit verse. Short, vivid pieces that told of the happiest moments, as well as the saddest. A portrait of a soul achingly in love, and in unspeakable pain."

Heaviness filled Julia's chest. A soul in love, and in unspeakable pain? A young woman whose beloved was cruelly torn from her? *Oh, Christopher.* Despite all Julia's efforts to contain her emotions this morning, tears were rising to her eyes again.

Margaret heaved a melancholy sigh. "But how do you know this Bharati wrote such poems," she asked, "if you're not even sure she existed?"

"Ah!" said Mr. Maji. "We still have the verses themselves. Each generation of the family has had at least one sympathetic soul who preserved them, and passed them down. They were never published, of course—even today, it would be considered shameful to have a female poet in the family who shared her work with the public. But Lady Eleanor and I have been working on a translation into English, which perhaps we may one day publish here in Britain, where it would be unlikely to cause embarrassment to my family back home."

"Goodness!" said Margaret. "I should love to hear one of the poems!"

"I can recite them," declared Eleanor. "One tends to remember them well after working out the translation. As I said, each one is very short—a cluster of heartfelt images, no more. This is one of the happier ones."

"Oh, yes," said Margaret. "A happy one, please!"

To Julia's surprise, Eleanor rose solemnly to her feet, and drew herself up as tall as such a stout little woman could manage. She took a deep breath, and then intoned:

Again, I met him in the woods,
Free there among the grazing deer.
He held me close in the shadows of the leaves,
Where I could scarcely see his face,
Where my fingers traced his handsome, dark body.

AND THAT, apparently, was the whole of it. Eleanor sat down again, folding her hands neatly in her lap, and the room was very quiet. A short cluster of images, she had said, and so it seemed to be.

Aunt Margaret had one hand pressed to her heart, and her mouth had fallen open. "Oh, dear!" she said, her cheeks glowing pink. "That is quite...*vivid* at the end there, is it not? At first, it sounded rather like Wordsworth, but then—"

Eleanor chuckled, relinquishing the dignified tone of her recitation. "Prakrit poets are quite frank about the pleasures of the body. But they can speak to the soul as well." Suddenly, she leaned across the space between her armchair and the divan and placed a hand on Major Holsworth's broad knee, patting it affectionately. "Marcus, dear," she said, "you remember that verse you were so fond of, the one you were so clever at helping me with as we were sailing here? About the darkness of night?"

Holsworth? Holsworth had helped Aunt Eleanor with a translation of an Indian love poem? Though given what he'd done with her in the hothouse room, perhaps it shouldn't be quite such a surprise. In any case, Julia hoped she wasn't gaping at him too openly.

Thankfully, the major seemed to be paying her no attention. He was, in fact, staring abstractedly into the cold fireplace, his thoughts entirely opaque, though he nodded in answer to Eleanor's questions.

To Julia's utter astonishment, he, too, began to recite, leaning forward with his forearms balanced on his knees, the words rolling out in his deep, vibrating voice:

When Night draws its black shadows across the sky,
Then comes the brightest light.
For then you draw back the curtains of my bed,
And the heat of your sun
Makes fire blaze within my breast.

AND NOW IT was Julia's turn to blush. Good heavens—beds and heat and breasts? Ought they to be reciting such shocking verses in an English parlor, so early in the morning?

Heat crept through her, nonetheless, as she imagined the

young poetess reclining on a heap of silken pillows, and a male hand pulling back the curtain that concealed her. She could see the man's dark shape in the shadows, lowering his body over his lover's.

And then she blinked, quite startled. The male face she saw her in mind as she imagined the scene—it was not Christopher's face.

It was *Holsworth's.*

Without her brain even giving a command to move, she jumped to her feet, her right hand clutching once again at the gold band that encircled her left wrist.

"Julia?" said Aunt Eleanor. "Are you quite all right?"

"Of course," she answered, perhaps a bit too quickly. "The verses are…remarkable, without a doubt. But, if I may ask, what does all this have to do with the *bracelet?*"

"Ah!" said Eleanor, smiling a mysterious smile. "Well, we have no direct proof of this, either, but the family stories go on to say that Bharati, in her endless grief, turned her attentions not only to the art of verse-making, but also to the art of enchantment."

"*Enchantment?*"

"The magic arts," confirmed Mr. Maji, giving Julia an assessing look from behind his gold-rimmed glasses. "They say she sought ways to help other young lovers avoid her sad fate. She wanted to help them find their hearts' desires, even when family or society would not approve."

"And, by one account at least, she was successful," said Eleanor. "That story claims she had a bracelet crafted all of gold, and imbued it with a charm that would draw true lovers together, and help them find happiness, despite all obstacles that might stand in their way."

Julia stared down at her wrist in shock. "And you think such a bracelet actually exists? You believe it is *this* bracelet?"

"It is a fanciful idea, to be sure," said Mr. Maji. "The

legend of the bracelet may be nothing more than a sentimental embellishment of Bharati's tale, by some later relative who wished to lighten the tragedy with the promise of new romance."

Julia's heart seemed to flip in her chest. "Surely, it is nothing more than that!"

The legend just *couldn't* be true. Magic of that sort didn't exist, not in the real world. And she and Holsworth were not true lovers. Aside from last night's burst of passionate madness, it made no sense for them to be lovers of any kind, at all.

Suddenly, though, the bracelet seemed almost to tingle against her skin, and her heart was hammering. She felt a desperate urge to twist violently at the metal, to bite through it if she had to, to get it off her wrist. She restrained herself, of course.

Eleanor was watching her very carefully now, with an impish gleam in her eye. "Perhaps I should tell you exactly how the bracelet came into my hands," she said. "It was about six months ago, when I was in Mr. Maji's aunt's library, looking through a drawer of old palm-leaf manuscripts. I lifted a lovely, illuminated section of the Bhagavata Purana which I'd quite been longing to read, and to my surprise, underneath it was that little sandalwood box. Mind you, many others had looked through that drawer over the years, and no one had reported finding a box before. Of course, I was even more startled to open the box and find such a valuable, exquisite bracelet inside!"

"It was indeed startling," said Mr. Maji. "I happened to be in the library as well, transcribing a work of Balinese philosophy, when Lady Eleanor called me over. We ended up spending days together, studying that inscription, comparing it to Bharati's own writings, and trying to piece together how the bracelet might have stayed concealed so long. I'm still not sure how something becomes *eternally yours when you give it away*, but I soon realized that working with Lady Eleanor on the project was without question the loveliest and most joyful time of my life."

The couple exchanged a beaming look, and reached out for one another's hands across the space between the armchairs.

Eleanor squeezed her husband's fingers fondly. "And if finding the bracelet made two gray-haired, stubborn, reclusive old bachelor scholars tumble madly into love," she said, "it must have enchantment of *some* kind."

His left hand still clasped in his wife's, Mr. Maji stretched his other arm towards Julia and touched his fingertips lightly to the bracelet. "And now, Lady Grantleigh, it seems Bharati's bracelet has chosen you."

Julia's cheeks went blazing hot. "Oh, ridiculous!" she said, springing backwards out of his reach. "I—I am not at all the type for star-crossed romance!"

"Are you sure?" His eyes twinkled.

"Quite sure. I am a widow now. Such things are—they *must* be—quite behind me."

Eleanor chuckled. "I thought something similar about myself. In fact—"

Whatever she was about to say was interrupted by a thumping noise from Holsworth's side of the divan. They all looked down to see that a little porcelain figurine of a King Charles spaniel that usually graced the end table had fallen and struck the carpet, apparently helped there by a bump from Holsworth's elbow.

Hastily, Holsworth snatched it up. It appeared to be unbroken. "Excuse me," he said, as he placed it back where it belonged. "I'm not really designed to fit in delicate spaces."

Big as a bull, Julia thought. And then immediately

clamped down on that thought. That was *not* the direction she needed her mind going just now.

Mr. Maji fixed the major once more with a scholarly, considering look. And then, suddenly, he, too, rose to his feet. "Enough of this academic chatter," he said. "It is a fine day outdoors. Perhaps we can all stroll in the gardens? I've never seen a proper English garden, except in paintings. I should be most gratified to make the acquaintance of a cowslip or a daffodil, if any are in residence right now."

"Oh," said Margaret, jumping up as well, still looking rather flustered by the poetry. "I'm sure we can find you something properly English in bloom."

"Sister Margaret," Mr. Maji said, holding out an elbow to her, "will you take one of my arms? My wife wishes to spend as much time in her sister's presence as she can while we are here, and I should be most happy to escort both of you together. Major Holsworth, I am sure you would be willing to escort Lady Grantleigh?"

Julia glanced at the major, and saw him square his jaw, as though preparing for an unwelcome duty.

"Of course," Holsworth said.

"But wait!" exclaimed Margaret. "Poor Julia never had a chance to touch her breakfast! Marcus, dearest, will you be sure she actually *eats* something before you bring her outdoors? I fear she'll flutter away in the wind if she doesn't."

Holsworth hesitated a moment before bowing his head in acquiescence. "You can depend on me," he answered somberly, Julia could not quite tell whether he was being jocular, or resigned.

As the gray-haired trio strolled out the French doors that led to the gardens, Christopher's two aunts on either side of Mr. Maji were giggling with their heads inclined towards one another. It was impossible to hear exactly what they were saying, but Julia thought she caught the words *lovers* and *romance*. Of course they were probably still talking about Bharati's verses, but she couldn't quite help feeling she was at the mercy of some sort of conspiracy.

Nonetheless, she did as she was bid, and returned to the breakfast room, sitting down dutifully long enough to force down some toast with cherry conserves. She ignored the coddled eggs. Holsworth stood guard over her, quite literally, drumming his fingers on the top rail of the nearest chair.

A hoot of laughter from Aunt Eleanor sounded on the other side of the breakfast room window. Apparently, they were taking their time in the China rose garden. "Oh, believe me, Margaret," came Eleanor's voice, quite loudly, perfectly audible even through the window glass. "It's never too late to embrace the pleasures of love! We may be long in the tooth, but we certainly still have appetites!"

The finger-drumming stopped, and Holsworth sighed wearily. "Lady Eleanor has been away from England a very long time. She forgets what topics are appropriate for polite conversation."

"Is it really any different from when you knew her as a boy?"

He laughed gruffly. "No, I suppose not. Though, back then, she'd never speak of such…sensual matters within my hearing. She had that much propriety, at least."

Such sensual matters. Oh, Lord. Was Holsworth's mind as distracted as hers was by the memories of what they'd done together on the hothouse divan? Or was he used to doing such things, with dozens of other ladies? Perhaps what happened between them, physically at least, had meant very little to him at all.

Julia took a hurried sip of her tea, which had gone cold and bitter and barely tolerable to swallow. She choked it down anyway.

Thankfully, Holsworth walked over to the window,

looking out over the garden, giving her a bit of breathing space. "I'm sorry if hearing those verses embarrassed you," he said, still facing away from her. "Bharati's poetry *is* beautiful, though—truly it is, and very moving, once you adjust your mind to the particular sensibility."

That made her put her teacup down, lest her suddenly unsteady hands slosh liquid all over the tablecloth. Just yesterday at this time, she'd thought of Holsworth—when she thought of him at all—as always stern, almost somber. She wouldn't have imagined him so skilled in the sensual arts. And she most certainly wouldn't have expected him to speak of the beauty of poetry, or the sensibilities of the mind.

She snuck a glance at him out of the corner of her eye. "I was a bit surprised to hear you reciting like that," she admitted. "I wouldn't have pegged you for a lover of poetry."

His expression went stiff. "No? I do have a Cambridge education, Lady Grantleigh." One eyebrow lifted. "And a soul."

Oh, Lord, and she'd insulted him again. Or so he thought. "I didn't mean it that way," she said. "Of course I know you have both." *Dash it all*—it sent a pang through her to have him speak so coldly to her again.

Though, of course, coldness between them was what she should *want*. The physical pull she felt towards him was still disconcertingly strong, and she couldn't risk tumbling into chaos again.

"Well," he said, turning to face her again, his eyes and voice both gone hard as flint. "As you said yourself, you are not at all the type for star-crossed romance."

Oh, yes, he was cold. Very, very cold.

And….*hurt*, perhaps?

Oh, dear. Perhaps he wasn't as unaffected as she thought by what they'd done together. Or perhaps her distressed response to Mr. Maji's story about the bracelet had simply wounded his masculine pride.

What on earth was going on inside his mind right now?

Heavens, have mercy. Much as she wanted to put last night behind them, she supposed they did need to speak about it, at least briefly. To clarify things.

To put it all safely behind them.

Pushing away her teacup, she rose slowly to her feet, crossing the few feet to join him at the window.

"Last evening," she began, softly, when she reached his side. "Last evening was a most unusual circumstance, one neither of us could have planned, or even foreseen. We both know that."

"So it was," he said, his face expressionless.

Her heart thumped. If only standing close to him did not make her feel she was weakening inside. Even now, some deep impulse made her want to lean into his body, to rest her head against his chest. But she had to try to keep her mind clear. Stay rational about all this.

"I want you to know, I am...*grateful* to you," she said. "For—for—" Oh, this was impossible. She broke off, fumbling for a tolerable way to phrase what she meant. "I am grateful that you were so compassionate to me last night, in a time of great need."

"Grateful?" He arched a skeptical brow at her, and his voice held a note of scorn. "*Compassionate?*"

She felt herself blush. Oh, Lord, Holsworth *did* seem angry, and hurt. And she had no idea what she was supposed to do about that.

Christopher had never been angry with her, ever, in all the years they'd spent together.

A wave of sadness washed through her chest, and—as had happened so many times before—she felt heavy with longing for her husband's steadiness, his warmth, his easy smile.

She squeezed her fingers tight together, tried to fight back another flood of tears. "I behaved badly last night," she said. "Selfishly. Thinking only of how our—our *interaction* affected me."

"*Interaction*? Is that what it is now?" His teeth ground together audibly.

"Please, Major Holsworth. You must understand. I *know* you understand," she insisted to the man standing so rigidly before her, "that I love Christopher. I am *Christopher's wife*, still. In my heart at least, even if he is gone."

There, that needed to be said. It was the truth, after all.

But why did her heart ache so badly now, as though it were being twisted at the root?

Holsworth seemed to have turned to stone. "I do understand," he said. "And Christopher deserves no less. I said as much last night."

"So," she said, feeling rather as though she were groping her way down an unfamiliar corridor in the pitch dark. "Last night was…a short burst of madness, as it were. Brought on by grief."

"Most certainly." His face gave away nothing of what he might be feeling. But, oddly enough, his eyes now made a quick, calculating sweep of the room, taking in the open doors to the kitchens and the parlor and the foyer hallway. "However," he said, switching suddenly to the crisp, authoritative tone she supposed he used as a battlefield commander, "there are some more practical matters we need to discuss. And we should not do that indoors, where the servants might overhear. Let us do as Mr. Maji instructs, and take a turn in the gardens."

Julia bit down on her lip. Of course Holsworth deserved

the chance to say whatever it was he felt he needed to say. She owed him that much, if not far more.

And outdoors was certainly far safer than any private place indoors for that to happen.

"As you wish," she said, and took his arm.

CHAPTER 8

*M*arcus clenched and unclenched his right fist, trying to master the restless discomfort that tensed his muscles as if he were headed into combat.

Which was…ridiculous. There was no battle to fight here, and he had no right to behave as he was behaving. He had no claim on Julia. He never had. He never would.

She'd made it perfectly clear she found it agonizing to have him under her late husband's roof after what passed between them last night. If there weren't urgent practical matters to discuss with her, the only decent thing for him to do would be to head straight to the Boar's Head and take the next mail coach back to London.

Unfortunately, there *were* urgent matters, and they couldn't be ignored. The burden of duty weighed on his chest like a slab of granite, pressing down against his lungs.

Fate offered him one small mercy, at least—when they walked out past the rose garden and onto the great rolling sweep of lawn that stretched down toward the village, Mr. Maji and Christopher's aunts had disappeared from view.

"Over here," he said, directing Julia up a flagstone path

that skirted the south side of the house, leading toward the wooded part of the estate. They could follow the walking path up the hill to the little Grecian folly, with its picturesque view of the river and surrounding valley, and its shielding marble walls. No one would overhear their conversation there.

"Oh," said Julia, tugging back on his elbow. "We won't find the others in that direction. Margaret never climbs. She complains too much of the stiffness in her hips and knees."

"I know. I have no wish to find the others. They mustn't hear what I have to say to you, any more than the servants should."

Julia stubbornly stood her ground. "But we're private enough right here, or if you don't think so, we can just go down into the apple grove." She gestured down a gentle side slope to a grassy area surrounded by a few dwarfish espaliered trees—a place where anyone looking out the southern windows of the house could see them clearly.

That slab of granite pressed down heavier and colder still.

Damnation. She was actively afraid of being alone with him.

"For pity's sake, Julia," he found himself growling. "Are you worried I'll try to draw you into my clutches again? Believe me, I'm aware my behavior last night was utterly inexcusable, and if you had any living male relatives, I'd happily let them take me out and shoot me."

She blinked in surprise. "Oh," she said, her cheeks flushing pink. "That's a bit melodramatic, don't you think? I don't view you as having *clutches*."

"But you want to ensure we remain in full view of others."

She heaved an exasperated sigh, and dropped her hold on his arm, pivoting to face him straight on. "I'm just trying to be sure we behave properly from now on," she said. "Let me repeat, Major, I blame only myself for what happened last night. I take full responsibility. I'm the one who kissed you, after all. And I refused to let you stop when you wished to."

He swallowed hard. Oh, how little she understood. *Do you really think I* wished *to stop? Never. Never. My own impulses were quite out of control.*

He shook his head. "I shouldn't have allowed it to happen at all," he insisted harshly. "You were overcome with emotion, and you'd never known anything but honorable marriage. I have far more experience of the world, and am at least *meant* to be a gentleman. So the responsibility was entirely mine."

"Great heavens!" Her brow furrowed now, and she crossed her arms over her chest. "You make me sound like a fool—like a mindless hoop knocked along by a stick. Do you think ladies can't control themselves, or discourage gentlemen who try to take things too far? Any girl out in Society learns how to fend off men trying to whisk her off for private assignations—a wedding ring doesn't discourage the more audacious ones, you know. You didn't take advantage of me, Major Holsworth, so get that noble thought right out of your mind. I was fully aware of what I was doing."

"You told me you thought you were going mad!"

"Not when I kissed you. By then, you'd reassured me there was nothing wrong with my mind, and I was—I was seeking to assuage my grief. Which I did. Which *you* did." Her cheeks glowed red as apples now, but her gaze was firm and steady. "And I needed that more than I know how to express. Given the same circumstances, I would make the same choice again."

He stared back at her for a long moment, entirely thunderstruck. "Very well, then, Lady Grantleigh," he said at last. "I will not insult you further with apologies."

"Good."

"To be clear, though, I do intend to behave honorably now." He straightened his shoulders. This next part of their conversation would be the bitterest, and his throat constricted as though fighting back a surge of gall. "I will respect whatever preferences you have, of course," he said. "But if it should become *necessary*—I mean, if there are, well, *physical consequences* of our actions—I hope you will consider accepting the protection of my hand and my name. For whatever they are worth."

Now she was the one who looked thunderstruck. "Physical consequences? You mean if—if I should find myself with child?"

"Yes," he said, scarcely able to draw air for the words. "Yes, that is what I mean."

"My husband and I shared a bed every night for six years, and despite our best efforts, I never conceived. I doubt there will be any cause to worry."

"Well, even if there are no practical concerns," he said, "if you should come to feel any *moral* compunction about what we have done—" He broke off, his pulse suddenly pounding, the rush of blood loud in his ears. "Regardless of the reason, if you should wish it, I offer you marriage under any terms acceptable to you."

A muscle twitched along her jaw. "Such a romantic proposal."

"It's not meant to be romantic. You've been quite clear about where your romantic loyalties lie."

That made her wince.

Blast it all, he'd rather face a cavalry charge than continue this conversation. But, of course, he never backed down from his duty.

"Since we are being perfectly honest with one another, Lady Grantleigh," he said, "I'll be the one to say it out loud: I'm well aware that marriage to a man like me is not something a woman like you should be expected to find acceptable except under the most desperate circumstances. We both know my name has not the tenth part of the value of the one you already possess."

Her eyes went very wide. "I'm sure I don't know what you mean, Major."

"Damn it!" Anger flashed hot through his chest. "You ask me not to treat you like a fool, Julia. Please do not treat me like one. I'm well aware what most of your social set thinks about men like me—ones who dare rise from the lowliest ranks to assume any position of authority in the world."

She said nothing, but she cast her gaze to the ground. Of course she understood what he meant. She was born the daughter of an illustrious earl, and had married another just as illustrious. She was a countess, at the very pinnacle of society. She knew her place in the world, and she knew his.

He spoke the words anyway, to ensure there could be no misunderstanding between them. And perhaps also out of a perverse sort of pride. "The Grantleighs are an exceptional family," he declared. "They opened their home to me, to the orphaned son of a lowly farmer. They secured me an education, and never made me feel that I was an intruder in their midst. I will always be grateful for that. I will always, for their sakes, do my best to behave like a gentleman, worthy of their kindness, if not their rank. But the rest of the world is not so kind. I'm well aware what most members of the *haut ton* say about me. I've heard all the jokes."

"*Jokes?*" she said, glancing up again. She seemed genuinely surprised. "What jokes?"

"About how the Grantleighs brought their livestock into the dining room to eat with them. That sort of thing."

"*What?*"

"I didn't say they were clever jokes."

"But that's—*horrid*! Who made such remarks? I've never heard anyone say anything of the sort!"

"They wouldn't say it to your face, my lady, or to any of the Grantleighs. You are too important to insult. But they find ways to let such comments slip just within my hearing. As a child, if I fell behind the family walking home from church, I could be sure some boy from one of the more genteel local families would seize the chance to fling mud at me, or try to push me into the river. And Lord knows, at Cambridge, I had to spend half my time behind the Pembroke kitchens pummeling some snot-nosed peer or other with my fists."

"You didn't! Christopher never told me any of that!"

"Christopher never saw it. And I never spoke of it to him." He flexed his hands now, remembering the bruised and split knuckles he'd so often concealed beneath fine kid gloves —gloves he'd never have owned in the first place without the generosity of the Grantleighs. "Eventually, my reputation for winning those fights brought me some measure of peace. And in the army, at least, most men have cared less about my parentage than my skill at keeping their hides intact. But get a few drinks in them, and the more well-born officers still joke as they please."

"Fellow *officers*? They wouldn't!"

"They *do*." He shrugged resignedly. "The simple fact, Lady Grantleigh, is that I will never truly belong in the circles in which I live."

Her eyes flashed with outrage. "How dare such men insult you!" she exclaimed. "You have more than proved yourself as an officer, as a *hero*!"

"You yourself called me a bull."

Her jaw fell. "I said you were as *big* as one. I was speaking metaphorically!"

"You were shocked I read poetry."

"Oh, that's unfair! I merely meant you never seemed the sentimental sort, not that you were a—a *barnyard animal*. I swear to you, if I ever *did* hear anyone suggest such a thing, I'd knock them down and scratch out their eyes!"

Her hands were balled into fists, her expression ferocious. She looked angry enough to round up the entire *haut ton* and give them all a sound beating for his sake.

Oh, Lord. Slim and delicate as she was, a good-sized kitchen cat could beat her in a fight, and yet she wanted to defend him against the most powerful people in the world.

And just like that, the wall of self-righteous indignation he'd been building up around himself for the last few minutes, perhaps the last few hours, probably for years and years before that, crumpled away to nothing.

"Oh, Julia," he said, drinking in the sight of her. A sudden, unaccountable bubble of mirth burst through him, and he found himself shaking with laughter. "Julia Grantleigh, you *are* formidable. And loyal to the core. And I swear, one day you will be the death of me."

She gaped at him, dumbfounded, and her fists unfurled. "Why on earth are you *laughing*?" she asked, a note of hurt in her voice. "And what do you mean, I will be the *death* of you? I was—I was trying to be supportive."

"I'm sorry," he said, clutching a hand to his abdomen, against the laughter rumbling there. "Yes, I know you were supporting me. Of course you were. You have always been the very best of women."

She still stared at him as though he'd turned lunatic.

And perhaps he had.

He thought he'd never seen her lovelier—standing there in the sunlight in her sweet yellow frock, the wind teasing black curls loose from her upswept hair. Her eyes still blazed, and her concern for him was vivid on her face.

She was so utterly beautiful.

And more than anything else he'd ever wanted before in his life, he wanted, achingly, desperately, to wrap her in his arms and kiss her again.

He sighed. The laughter stopped dead inside him.

Of course he *wasn't* going to kiss her. He had more than enough regrets from the previous night, and honor wouldn't allow him to draw Julia further into something that could only end in disaster for her.

But he gave himself a moment, just a moment more, to gaze at her.

Then he reached deep for the reins of self-discipline.

"Come now," he said soberly. "Let us walk on up the hill to the folly. It's time I told you something more, and it would be best if you had a place to sit down."

CHAPTER 9

*J*ulia felt dizzy, and it wasn't just from the exertion of the climb.

It was the man beside her.

Every moment spent in his presence seemed to spin her round faster, until she could scarcely be sure her feet were touching the ground. Each time they spoke, he revealed yet another unexpected layer of himself. And the more he revealed, the deeper he worked his way into her heart.

He'd always seemed so fierce to her, so impenetrably strong, it never occurred to her he'd once been a little boy coming home spattered in mud, or a young scholar having to defend his dignity with fistfights when men like Christopher could be happily at peace with their books.

The very thought unleashed a fury in her that she didn't know how to contain.

And, *dash it all*, it made her want to throw her arms around him and pull him close to her breast and whisper soothing words into his thick, dark hair.

And that…well, that led to other thoughts of what might happen if she pulled him close. Very dangerous thoughts, especially considering they were quite alone up here on the hill, where no one could see them.

Oh, great heavens—what was she going to do about him?

She'd meant what she told him earlier, that she still loved Christopher. She *did*. She couldn't imagine she would ever stop loving her husband. And yet this man…this man…

Was it possible—*could* it be possible, for one heart to open itself, to care so deeply, for two men at the very same time?

That thought made her dizzier than ever.

To her relief, he said nothing more to her as he led the way up through the stately elms and white-flowering rowan trees that lined the path to the folly. She hurried to keep up with his long strides, fighting to master the turmoil inside her. Whatever it was he needed to say, whatever required the distance and privacy of the woods, she owed it to him to listen with her full attention.

At long last, they reached the little clearing where a former Earl of Grantleigh had built his own miniature, half-ruined Greek temple—three pairs of fluted Corinthian columns around an arched doorway, leading into a chapel-like space with a domed roof. Artful holes were knocked in the marble here and there to let in streams of sunlight and fresh breezes, and allow English lords and ladies to imagine they'd stumbled upon some fabled, long-lost grove of Arcady.

On summer evenings, she and Christopher had often strolled up to sit under the arch and watch flocks of starlings fill the sky above the valley, flying in their shimmering, pulsating, twisting formations.

They thought they'd have a lifetime to share such sights together.

Since Christopher died, she hadn't had the heart to come here, and her knees felt a little weak as she approached the spot. But Holsworth didn't stop at the threshold; he ushered her through the doorway beneath the arch, into the more shadowy space inside.

The hush of it, at least, was as soothing as it had ever been, the heavy marble shutting out the noise and worries of the rest of the world. Along the walls, graceful carved maidens in flowing Grecian gowns formed pillars lifting up the small dome, their serene faces utterly untroubled by time.

For once, Julia envied the carvings, so certain of their place in the universe. They knew exactly where they should be, what they should do, today, tomorrow, forever.

A restless pulse went through her and she turned—and was surprised to find Holsworth closer behind her than she expected.

Good Lord. Did he not understand how the sheer size and strength of his body affected her? A sort of dark current seemed to urge her towards him, as though he were able to pull her close without so much as touching her with a fingertip. Perhaps he felt it, too, for his gaze locked on her eyes, and the rhythm of his breath rising and falling matched itself to hers.

For a moment, she felt suspended, her body wavering.

If he kissed her again now, she wouldn't resist. Far from it —she would give herself over completely, let him lift her in his arms, let him back her against the wall if he wanted. Sweet longing rushed through her, to have him do exactly that, to lift her skirts and urge her legs to wrap around his waist, and, *oh*, to push himself inside her as he had last night, so impossibly large and thick and hard, to fill her so completely, and drive her to that perfect state of ecstasy once more.

A hot blush swept over the whole surface of her skin. What a wanton she had become.

But Holsworth didn't kiss her. Far from it.

Just when she thought he might lean closer, he took a

step backwards instead. His hand indicated one of the long marble benches built into the walls. "You should sit down," he said.

And, at that, the sensual spell was broken. Equal parts shaken and relieved, she did as she was told. Holsworth, though, remained standing, looming over her, dark and ominous as a mountain.

And silent as one, too.

Something in his eyes told her he was struggling with whatever it was he had to say. For heaven's sake—what topic could possibly be more delicate, or more painful, than the conversation they'd already had this morning, with his rather surly offer of marriage should the *physical consequences* require it?

Holsworth paced a few steps back and forth now, fists behind his back, his face bent in shadow. He seemed quite deliberately to be avoiding the shafts of sunlight that shot through the holes in the roof, as though he didn't want to reveal more of himself than he absolutely had to.

Why? What was so difficult about what he had to tell her?

Or was he trying to *keep* something from her? Her pulse thrummed a little faster.

At last, Holsworth planted his feet again, and said, "You know my return to England this time was quite sudden."

"Quite sudden," she echoed.

"I did so to attend to an urgent and complicated matter." He paused, and swallowed audibly. "Involving one of your near neighbors."

She startled. "My neighbors?" The *neighbors* had drawn Holsworth all the way from India? "Which neighbors?"

He fell silent again. It seemed to require some effort to bring up any further speech. "Brayles," he said at last.

"Brayles?" Good grief—was she going to have to repeat

back each small fragment he gave her before he would grant her any more?

Holsworth heaved a sighed. "George Brayles, specifically," he said, and now his voice held a distinct note of distaste. "The Honorable George Cuthbert Brayles, who left Devonshire for India three years ago, bringing his unmarried sister and two young daughters with him."

She blinked a few times. *George Brayles*? The utterly unexceptional, boring George Brayles? The most interesting thing the man had ever done was to light out for foreign shores, and she'd heard nothing of note of him since. "What about George Brayles?"

Despite the shadows obscuring Holsworth's face, the intensity of his gaze on her was palpable. "How well would you say you know him?" he asked.

"Moderately well, I suppose," she said cautiously. "He's brother to Viscount Edgerton, of course, and, before he went abroad, a frequent guest at Grantleigh Hall. But surely you knew him better than I ever could, having grown up here at Grantleigh yourself."

"I'd prefer to hear your more recent impressions."

What on earth was Holsworth up to? His expression—what she could make out of it through the gloom—was awfully grave.

"I have very little to say about him," she said. "I was friendly with his wife, Caroline. You wouldn't remember her; they married while you were in India yourself. And, well—poor thing—she died soon after their second girl was born. But as for George, all I can call to mind just now is that striking auburn shade of his hair, and a rather unpleasant habit of getting cross with partners during games of whist."

Abruptly, Holsworth laughed. "An apt description, my lady. May I ask if you know *why* he came to India?"

"To seek his fortune, I presume." An irritable pressure

was building along her temples. "He's a fourth son who made only a modest marriage, and he has those two little daughters to support. He didn't seem cut out for the church or army, and when Caroline died…well, I believe he was rather at loose ends for a time."

"He took her death hard?"

"Why wouldn't he? Caroline was the sweetest of souls." Julia sighed. True, there'd been some talk among the servants that, after he lost his wife, Brayles perhaps took to drinking more heavily than was his wont, but that was nothing unreasonable for a grieving widower, and, in any case, not the sort of gossip a lady carelessly passed on. "Good heavens, Holsworth. Why on earth are you putting me through this interrogation? Did you have some dealings with George Brayles in India?"

Holsworth paused again, then slowly nodded. "As it happens, we crossed paths in Calcutta. I will not say we socialized—he was one of the mud-slingers when we were boys in Devonshire—but I was aware of his comings and goings."

Her brows flew up. "*Brayles* threw mud at you? How dare he!"

Holsworth waved a dismissive hand. "It's not his boyhood behavior that concerns me. From what I saw in India…well, let us just say the Honorable George Cuthbert Brayles is not entirely honorable."

"Not *entirely* honorable?" Her hands twisted impatiently in her lap. "Please, Holsworth. I beg you to speak more plainly. Did Brayles commit some outrage against you overseas?"

Holsworth blew out a long, hard breath and at last came to sit beside her on the bench, propping his fists on his knees.

His sudden nearness sent a fresh wave of unsettling

feeling through her. His body seemed at once alien and all-too-familiar. A bright stream of sunlight fell upon him now through a hole in the ceiling just above them, but it somehow only made his hair seem more black, the set of his face more fierce and immobile.

He turned towards her, regarding her somberly, and the impact of his gaze at such close quarters sent a shiver through her.

"Very well, Lady Grantleigh," he said. "I shall speak plainly indeed. Brayles, I fear, is a thoroughly black-hearted villain."

"A *what*?"

To Julia's surprise, Holsworth reached his hand toward hers as if about to clasp her fingers, but it stilled in the air at the last moment, then retreated again. "A villain," he repeated sternly. "And it's not his behavior toward me that I'm concerned with. Instead, I believe he may pose a particular danger to *you*."

Now her mouth fell open in surprise. "A danger to *me*? George *Brayles*? Good Lord, the only harm he's ever done me is trampling on my slipper in the midst of a yuletide ball. He might do damage to a leg of mutton, but never to me!"

"Hear me out," said Holsworth, and the fingers that had so nearly touched hers began drumming out an urgent rhythm against the top of his leg. "I suspect Brayles came to India not so much to improve his fortune as to save himself from very dire straits indeed."

"What do you mean? What sort of dire straits?"

"Financial ones," said Holsworth. "He and daughters and the unmarried sister who accompanied them arrived in an oddly shabby state for close relations to a viscount."

The pressure at her temples was growing painful, beating along with her pulse. "Oh, don't be absurd. Lord Edgerton is a generous man, and has always cared very well for his relatives."

"I tell you, it did not look it, not for George. His clothes, and those of his daughters and sister, were at least a season out of date, and the only ornament worn by any of them was a ruby heirloom ring Brayles wore on his little finger."

Julia frowned. That detail was one small anchor in what seemed to be an ocean of odd claims. "Yes, I know that ring —he often boasted how it passed down through his forefathers from the time of Queen Elizabeth."

"Precisely." Holsworth's fingers were drumming still, drumming relentlessly, as though some unaccountable anger were building in force within him.

Their motion made Julia oddly self-conscious of her own fingers, and she balled them tightly to keep them from twitching.

"I tell you, my lady," Holsworth said, "George Brayles must have fallen out of his brother's favor somehow before he left England. Are you sure you heard nothing of the sort?"

Goodness, Holsworth was behaving as though his concerns were very serious indeed. If Christopher were here now, what would Christopher tell him?

Christopher trusted Holsworth. Christopher would have me say something.

"Well," she said tentatively. "One hears things. After Caroline passed, George was perhaps not quite as moderate as he should have been in—in drink." Embarrassment heated her throat. "But—but he'd just suffered a great loss, and I suppose one must allowances."

The lines of Holsworth's face grew even more severe. "Perhaps his brother the viscount did not make allowances. Edgerton was a military man before he inherited the title, you know. He puts great stock in honor, and has been known to be quite strict."

"Well, yes. But…what of that? You must spell this out more clearly for me. You believe Brayles was in financial difficulties when he arrived in India? And this concerns *me* somehow?"

Holsworth nodded. "I kept an eye out for him in Calcutta, for his family's sake, if not for his. It soon became quite clear he had no skill at insinuating himself into profitable business ventures. His clothing only became shabbier, and, far worse, he began frequenting certain less than savory establishments the soldiers enjoy for strong drink and gambling—hoping, I assume, to rebuild his fortunes at the gaming tables."

"*And?*"

"And one day the ruby ring was gone from his finger."

She blinked. Now that was a telling detail—Brayles had truly treasured that ring. "Gambled away?"

Holsworth nodded. "He was no better a card sharp than he was a businessman, I'm afraid. And no doubt he was frantic at the loss—that ring was his family pride and joy. I have connections of my own in Calcutta, and I set out to see if I might intercede on his behalf, again for the sake of his family. I have always respected Edgerton, and hated to see his family's honor sullied. It wasn't hard to get the story, or to discover ledgers at multiple establishments recording the tremendous debts George Brayles had racked up all over town, drawing on the credit of his brother's good name."

Debts? Julia's cheeks were hot now, as well as her throat. It felt all wrong to be discussing a gentleman's private behavior in this way. Especially a gentleman from the neighborhood, a man who had often been a guest at the Grantleigh table.

"Oh, but come now, Holsworth," she insisted. "We ought not to be talking in these terms. Gambling debts are an occupational hazard for the younger brothers of viscounts, as is excessive fondness for drink. If you come racing back from India every time an Englishman displays those common vices, you shall become permanently seasick. Brayles may be a wastrel, but how does any of this make him a black-hearted villain?"

"That has to do with the man who won the ring from him. That man was a former military officer of the East India Company who'd resigned his post after losing a leg in battle. He then commenced, by some mysterious means, to make himself a fortune running a Calcutta tea shop."

"A *tea* shop?" The story only grew more muddled. "For goodness sake," she said. "What sort of old sailor's yarn are you spinning here?"

"Do you not see the oddity, Lady Grantleigh? A tea shop might make a man a modest living, but it is too small a business to generate great fortune. And, in fact, that is not where the man's money came from. The army was quite aware the tea-shop owner had taken up another shadow trade of a far more nefarious nature—he'd fallen in with agents of the Peshwa, the Maratha ruler who was preparing to make war on the British. In rooms behind the tea shop, the man traded in opium and stolen goods, and used the silver he gained to procure foreign weapons he could sell in turn to the Peshwa's Pindari fighters."

The significance of *that*, at least, she understood. "A British officer selling weapons to the enemy! Well, that's treason! Great heavens—why did the army not shut the tea shop down?"

Holsworth shrugged. "The weapons were inferior to those the British had, anyway, and knowing the operation's exact location gave our spies a convenient means of keeping track of other things being communicated between the Peshwa and his followers in Calcutta."

"Oh!" she said. "That's rather devious!"

"Espionage generally is."

"But . . ." Her head was wheeling a bit by now. "What can all that possibly have to do with George Brayles?"

"Scarcely a week after I noticed the ruby ring was gone, it was back on Brayles' finger."

"He got it back? Perhaps he simply got luckier at the gaming tables."

"His suits of clothes improved remarkably at nearly the same time, and his sister began to dress in the best of Indian-made fashion. They procured quite an elegant house in the best area of the city, and when I went to examine the ledgers of his debts again, everything had been paid off—many, many thousands of pounds, in the course of a single week. Enough for them to have lived on for years, had he actually possessed all that money in the first place."

An uncomfortable feeling began to creep into her stomach. "Perhaps he got much, *much* luckier at the tables."

Holsworth gave her a measured, meaningful look. His eyes seemed very black.

"You think he—" She broke off. So very much money. So soon after getting in the debt of an unscrupulous traitor. But Brayles was a man who'd sat often at Christopher's table, whose infant daughters she'd bounced on her knee. She sat at church every Sunday across from one of his aunts, a staunchly religious widow, and took tea with his kind-hearted sister-in-law, who still wept sometimes when they spoke of poor Caroline. "You think Brayles got all that money from the—the *tea-shop* man?"

"I cannot imagine it came from anywhere else."

She recoiled from the idea, horrified. It just couldn't be possible. Brayles might be an unpleasant man, but he was from *Devonshire*. From decent people. People she knew and loved well. "But why should you assume anything nefarious at all?" she said. "Perhaps one of Brayles' failing business ventures suddenly paid off. Perhaps he invested in the

Exchange back home, and earned a sudden dividend, or Lord Edgerton had a good report of him, or—or took pity on his poor young nieces, and provided a more generous allowance. I've even heard of men who believed themselves ruined, whose fortunes turned entirely when a ship thought lost at sea came safely home to port!"

"Perhaps, my lady. But—"

"And why would the tea-shop man wish to give him so much money anyway—as you say, many, many thousands of pounds? To a shabbily-dressed fellow with nothing to his own name but a ring on one finger?"

"Brayles was no longer shabby once he had the money, remember. And as soon as he looked the part of a wealthy viscount's brother, he was suddenly much sought out by what passes for British society in Calcutta. Most of the men of the East India Company—stunningly wealthy though some of them may be—are commoners by blood. And one thing they crave nearly as much as riches is the chance to elevate their place in society. Once it was clear George Brayles was a man of rank and status, he was much in demand for private dinners, for cognacs and cigars in the officers' clubs, for tête-à-têtes with high-ranking officials. With men known to drink heavily among their friends. Men who knew the secret inner workings of the government and of trade." His expression hardened. "And who knew the plans and strategies of the East India Company's military."

Julia hung on his words, her eyes widening. "You can't possibly mean to imply that—"

"That Brayles was in the employ of a man who could turn enormous profit selling British secrets to the Peshwa, but who lacked the social connections to learn those secrets himself? A man who would pay Brayles generously to pass such secrets along? That Brayles was desperate enough for money to agree? It certainly looks that way to me."

"Good God!" She jumped up from her seat, her heart throbbing, and her head going light. "You really mean it! You're accusing George Brayles of spying for the *enemy*! Of being a *traitor*!"

"You believed it easily enough of the tea-shop man! Is that because he wasn't a viscount's brother?"

Her cheeks burned. "You think I'm reacting out of snobbery? I don't *know* the tea-shop man! George Brayles was a guest in my *home*! I—I *danced* with him at parties! The Grantleighs and the Brayles have been friends and neighbors for at least three hundred years! He might be a disagreeable fellow at times, but a *traitor to the crown*?"

"Is he such a good friend to you? A few minutes ago, all you remembered was how rude he could be to card partners."

"Well, I remember more now." She hugged her arms tight against her ribs, fighting down a terrible feeling of nausea. It *couldn't* be true. She couldn't bear for such a thing to be true. "For heaven's sake, Holsworth—I stood near George Brayles at Caroline's funeral. The man wept like a baby!"

"You think traitors cannot weep?" Now Holsworth sprang to his feet, closing in on her, his eyes flashing. "You must listen to me, Julia. A man in my profession who's spent years in Calcutta gets a sense of these things, and—"

"A sense? You have a *sense* that Brayles is guilty of—of selling his nation's secrets to a foreign power? What *proof* of this do you have? Surely you have some solid proof?? More than just ledgers showing he was once in debt? More than just the temporary disappearance of a ring? For all you really know, he may simply have taken it to a jeweler to have the setting repaired!"

"*Julia*—"

She stood her ground, balling her hands into fists and jutting out her chin. "Tell me right now, Holsworth: do you or do you not have some *direct* evidence linking Brayles to the tea-shop man?"

Holsworth hesitated. "Traitors selling secrets tend not to keep elaborate records of their crimes. But I can certainly infer—"

"Stop!" she cried. She backed away now, as far away from him as she could go, until her spine bumped one of the marble maidens that held up the roof. "Just stop!"

Her brain didn't seem to be functioning properly. The bright sunlight pouring down through the gaps in the walls was suddenly dazzling, by contrast making the shadowed places beneath the dome seem darker than before. It gave her the feeling she was sinking deeper and deeper into a hole.

"George Brayles is a *gentleman*," she said at last, slowly and deliberately. "An accusation such as you are making would ruin him, ruin his family name, ruin his brothers and his sisters, people who are my friends. I am not saying he could not possibly be guilty of such awful things. But if you're going to say so, and if you're planning to take some action about it, a *sense* is not enough. An inference is not enough. You must have *proof*. Unassailable proof!"

Holsworth made a sound like a growl. "Poor men hang every day with far less *proof*! For pity's sake, Julia, are you defending Brayles simply because he's a member of your class?"

"Do you *suspect* him simply because he's a member of my class?"

Holsworth froze. "What is that supposed to mean?"

"Oh, God." She remembered something else, and it made her stomach sink. "Brayles was at Cambridge, wasn't he, when you and Christopher were there? If he threw mud at you as a boy, I can't imagine he treated you much better at university. Did he?"

Holsworth stared at her, his face still as stone.

"*Did* he?" Her thoughts were swirling madly. So much had passed between her and Holsworth in the past few hours, she'd felt so *close* to him, and yet she didn't really know him at all, did she? And now the words he was saying were tearing at the very fabric of the life she'd known here at Grantleigh Hall. Anger surged through her, dizzing and hot, and made her vision start to blur. "Did Brayles treat you well when you were at university?"

"No," Holsworth admitted, his voice tight, his jaw stiff. "No, he made it his business to ensure everyone I came in contact with knew the sordid details of my origins."

"And you must have hated him for that."

"Admittedly, I did. Of course I did."

"Of course." The muscles of her hands and legs began to shake. "You must hate him still. Is that what this is all about? Is it? These accusations against him?" Even as she said the words, she knew she might be going too far, might be entirely unjust for saying so, but the words came out anyway, angry and harsh and desperate. "Have you, at long last, found a way to get revenge?"

Holsworth's shoulders jerked, and his eyes drained of light. The air felt suddenly cold, and the marble floor between them might as well have cracked in a fissure a mile deep.

Oh, damn it all.

Everything about this felt horrid and wrong. The world felt off-kilter.

And all at once, the wild pendulum of her thoughts swung abruptly the other way. Such a short while ago, she'd been defending Holsworth, horrified that he'd been mistreated by officers and gentlemen, and now here she was, attacking him, accusing him of the basest sort of behavior.

That wasn't right. That just couldn't be right. Holsworth might be mistaken about Brayles, might have frightfully misjudged his behavior in India, but she knew Holsworth wasn't a scoundrel at heart, he wasn't a petty man.

Christopher had trusted him. Christopher had always said Holsworth was a deeply honorable man.

Suddenly she wished she could snatch her accusation back from the air and swallow it up again. "I'm sorry, Holsworth," she said, stretching out her hand. "I didn't mean...I only meant..."

He backed out of her reach. "You meant that you trust Brayles more than you trust me."

"No! Of course not." She pressed her hands to her temples—the pressure there had built suddenly to pain. "But listen, please. I—I know you would not act from selfish motives. But I am not wrong to want some concrete proof. Brayles may lack the charm and intelligence of his older brothers, but from all I know of him, he's just a—he's an ordinary man. Not evil. Not even...*clever* enough to do the thing you say he's done. How can you know what you're claiming is true?"

"You live in a golden tower, Lady Grantleigh!" Holsworth bit out the words, his expression almost cruel, and though he came no closer, the sound of his voice made her crouch tight as she could against the wall. "Nothing in the real, dirty world touches you, does it? But I live in that real world—the dirty, ugly, messy world where, *yes*, ordinary men like Brayles do unspeakable things, every bloody day, and hide it with their money and their power and—"

"Holsworth!" This was all becoming too much. Her husband had never so much as raised his voice to her, in all the years they spent together, much less spoken to her in such terms. "You forget yourself!"

"Bloody *hell*, Julia! You're as naïve as Christopher was."

It was as if he'd slapped her. "What are you talking about? *Christopher*? Christopher wasn't naïve—"

"Oh, God!" He advanced on her now, his eyes blazing. "You wanted to know what we argued about on that night when you heard us shouting at each other? *This* what we argued about. I'd written letters sharing my suspicions about Brayles, but they hadn't swayed him, so I took leave and came all the way to England to beg him in person to intervene, before Brayles cost the lives of British troops." Holsworth broke off, raking one hand roughly through his hair, looking as though his skull hurt as much as hers did. "He wouldn't believe me any more than you will."

"What?" He'd told Christopher all this, and Christopher didn't believe him?

Cold spread through her limbs again.

Holsworth loomed over her, his voice low and harsh. "I showed him the ledgers," he said. "A thick stack of them, showing Brayles' debts and their sudden repayment, plain as day. But Chris wanted to come up with more innocent explanations—just as you do. Christopher was a theorist, an idealist. Everything was philosophical to him. If he knew anything about what really happens in India—"

"Christopher *knew*. He studied everything he could get his hands on, spoke to every officer who returned, corresponded with officials, read dispatches every day! He devoted his life to—"

Holsworth slammed a fist against the marble wall, just a few feet from her head. "He never set *foot* there!"

That brought her up short. Anger flared again, hot and sore just behind her breastbone. It was one thing to accuse her of naiveté, but to insult *Christopher*—that was intolerable. "Christopher *couldn't* set foot there. The doctors said his heart couldn't stand the strain of the heat and travel. That wasn't his fault! But he knew all there was to know."

And Christopher hadn't believed the accusation against George Brayles.

She was shaking again, harder than before. Her thoughts were a whirlpool inside her, contradictions rushing hard in opposite directions until her head spun.

"Tell me this, Major Holsworth," she insisted, as a last logical piece fell into place in her mind. "Why was it necessary to come all the way back to England in the first place? There are British officials all over Calcutta. Could none of them *intervene*, as you say? If your case against Brayles was so persuasive—if the truth of it would be obvious to anyone who lived in India, to anyone who *understood* India—why did you not find help right there, right then?"

Oh, she'd touched a raw nerve now—the muscles of his mouth screwed up, his fingers speared again through his hair, almost tearing it this time. He cast his eyes downward, and opened and shut one fist convulsively as though struggling to master himself.

"I did try," he said after a long pause, clearly tamping down his anger and measuring out his words with care. "But the officers of the East India Company were not inclined to have their aristocratic friend questioned. Several of his new drinking companions vouched for his good character—as if they knew anything about the man. I could not get anyone in the city to listen."

"They didn't believe you." Fury pushed her on, now, making her insides ache. "Perhaps because you misjudged Brayles. The officers were right, and *Christopher* was right, and you're too prideful to admit that you were wrong! You'd rather have me believe my husband was a fool than—"

"I am not wrong about this, Julia!"

"Aren't you?" She was trembling from head to foot now, a dozen emotions coursing through her, clotting up together in her chest, in her throat—all her anger, and confusion, and guilt, and grief. "Is this about reason, or about resentment? I think perhaps you wish to hurt a man who once hurt you. Brayles. And maybe Christopher, too!"

"*Christopher*? Why on earth would I—"

"Why wouldn't you resent him? He was to the manor born. Everything came easily to him. No one ever threw mud at him, or muttered insults where he could hear them, or questioned his word about anything. It's natural enough that you would feel jealous of—"

"Dear God, Julia! Stop!" Holsworth strode to the other side of the little room, clamping his fists over his ears as though her words were physically painful to him. "You have no idea what you're saying!"

"Why?" she said, fiercely. An abyss was opening before her, terrifying and cold. She could feel herself begin to fall, but she couldn't seem to stop moving forward. "Why does it bother you? Because it's true?"

"Damn all that to hell! None of that matters to me. All that matters is keeping you safe."

"From what?"

"From Brayles," he said. "Brayles knows he's guilty, even if you don't. He knows with the war over, and captured Pindari being made to talk, a case may be built against him after all, a very damning case even a viscount's brother could swing for. He wants to erase all evidence that may point to his crimes. He wants the ledgers I gave to Christopher."

"Ridiculous," she said, but she felt an odd pulse of fear. "How would he even know the ledgers are here?"

"Christopher *told* him."

"*What*?"

"Brayles approached me one day in Calcutta, not long ago. He told me he'd received a letter from the earl. It seems Christopher's good conscience required him to inform Brayles that I'd seen the record of his debts, that I'd brought them with me to Grantleigh Hall. You know how honest

Chris was, how noble. He felt Brayles had a right to know how his behavior was being perceived. Being *misperceived*, as Christopher understood the situation. He wanted to be sure Brayles kept to the straight and narrow from then on." Holsworth shook his head. "And now I fear that letter might get you killed. Brayles is coming for the ledgers. I know he is."

Julia stared at Holsworth long and hard, trying to read his expression. But where he stood, a beam of sunlight just past his shoulders threw the bulk of his body into silhouette. His face, turned halfway toward her, was cast in harsh relief, part blindingly bright, part in deep shadow. He might as well have been one of the marble carvings.

A wave of exhaustion washed over her. She wanted to go back, to turn everything back, to last night when he was so warm and tender with her, when his eyes had seemed kind and his motives clear.

"This is madness, Holsworth," she said. "I cannot let you go on like this."

"You cannot ask me to leave. Not now. Brayles and his family disappeared from India just before I did. No one seems to know where they were heading, only that they were gone."

"What of that? They might be going anywhere."

"He's coming here." Holsworth's voice was dark, and so certain.

Her confidence wavered.

"I'm telling you, Julia," he said. "I feel it in my gut. The Peshwa's kingdom is falling apart, and the rats are rushing out from the woodwork, eager to sell whatever scraps of information they can. Brayles is afraid of being exposed, and *he's coming here.*"

She shook her head desperately. "I don't understand why you're doing this, Holsworth. You're angry at this man and men like him, resentful of the way you were treated as a boy. It was unfair and horrible of them, but that does not make Brayles a traitor and—and a would-be *murderer* now."

Holsworth's hands sliced the air in what looked like severe frustration. "Forget the way I was treated as a boy! Bloody hell, Julia, I'm not doing this because of Brayles, or Christopher, or any other man!"

"Then *why*?"

Holsworth went very still, the only part of him in motion the harsh rise and fall of his chest as his breath roared from his lungs. He closed his eyes as if in agonizing pain. "I'm doing it because…because…"

"*Why*?"

"Good God, Julia, don't you understand?" He sounded utterly miserable. "Isn't it obvious yet?"

"Nothing about this is obvious."

"Damn it all, Julia! I'm doing it—I'm doing it because I love you."

The world reeled around her. "What?"

"I *love* you. I have always loved you."

Always? She waited, paralyzed, willing his words to resolve themselves into some other, different form, some other meaning than the one she had just heard. "You can't mean that."

"I do mean it." All the furious tension seemed to drain from his body now—his fists uncurled, his shoulders slumped. "I never said a word about it because—because you belonged to Chris. You loved him, and it was clear you were the center of his world. I wouldn't have tried to come between you."

She shook her head disbelievingly. "You couldn't have come between us."

"I don't deny that."

"I don't understand this—you loved me when I was *married*? While I was Christopher's *wife*?"

"I loved you before you were married," he said, his voice bleak. "From the first time I laid eyes on you." Astonishingly, he took a step closer, not crowding her this time, but stepping forward just enough to allow him to reach out his arm and run a finger across the rim of her bracelet. "And you never would have known, Julia, if it weren't for this—this damnable *troublemaker* around your wrist."

Then he swung away, and turned his back on her, becoming a dark shadow once more.

Dear God, how could she ever have felt numb in her life —waves of pain and shock coursed through her now, so strong and relentless she felt they might tear her open. All the edges of her world were fraying, unraveling at once.

And she was the one who'd let it happen, who'd made the first tear in the fabric last night, when she'd kissed Holsworth. When she'd given in to the weakness of her body.

That had been her fault.

That had been her mistake.

She gripped the edge of the bracelet with the fingers of her other hand and gave a ferocious tug, wishing she'd never slid it on her wrist, never found the thing.

"Well," she said bitterly to the man standing before her, "You've had me now, haven't you?"

And then another horrible thought struck her. "Oh, sweet heaven, you knew about the *poetry*," she said. "About Bharati's poetry. You helped Eleanor with the translations. She must have told you the tale. Did you—did you know about the *bracelet* as well? Did *you* put it in my room, knowing I'd hear that story? Did you think me such a sentimental fool that I'd swallow that fable whole and let it delude me into falling in love with you?"

"What?" He whirled back to face her now, his face

incredulous. "*No*—I was out on campaign when Eleanor and Mr. Maji met. They were married and on their honeymoon before I returned to the city. I never saw that bracelet...never heard a word about it until you did. I have no idea how the blasted thing got into your room."

Could she believe him, or not? Could she even trust her own senses at this point? Everything was jumbled, scattered, broken into pieces. "I think you should leave now, Holsworth. I think you should leave and never see me again."

His fists tightened again. "Oh, God, Julia. Is it so unforgivable, that I should love you?"

"Of course it's unforgivable!" she cried, and she knew the accusation had to be directed against herself as well as him, after what she'd done with him last night. "I was *Christopher's wife*. He might as well have been your brother."

"Julia, please. Hate me if you like, but don't ask me to leave. Not now. Brayles will—"

She shook her head frantically. "I don't care. I don't care if he's a villain. I don't care if he's coming. You have no right —no right to protect me. I am the Countess of Grantleigh, and I will take care of myself."

Holsworth took one step forward, his eyes locking on hers.

He didn't speak, he just stared at her for a long moment, an excruciating moment, and in that space of time, she felt the pull of him again, felt that weakening deep within her, a mad impulse that said she *shouldn't shouldn't shouldn't* send him away, that if she had any sense at all, she would throw her arms around him and cling tight and beg him not to leave her.

It would be so easy—easy as falling from the top of a staircase after a single, soft push.

But she wrenched herself backward, remembering who and what she was.

"Go," she said. "Just go."

Holsworth stood fast, his eyes still boring into hers, so black and fathomless and unyielding. "I'm sorry, Julia. I can't do that."

"Then *I* will go," she said, taking a step towards the arch-way. "And if you try to block my path, I will scream. I'll scream so loud, they'll hear me down in the valley."

He didn't move.

So she darted past him and ran as fast as she could down the hill, trying not to remember her last sight of him, and the agony she saw in his eyes.

CHAPTER 10

*J*ulia rushed through the servants' entrance and up the back stairway so she wouldn't have to speak to anyone. When she reached her chamber, she shoved the door shut behind her and collapsed at the foot of her bed, without strength even to lift the covers and crawl inside.

Anger and guilt twisted and curled inside her, burning and icy all at once—she felt betrayed, and also somehow that she'd committed a horrific betrayal, and she couldn't sort out who was to blame.

So she lay there, curled in a ball, gripping her knees against her chest, while the beams of the afternoon sun made their full, slow circuit across the length of the room, deepening into the heavy gold of end of day, and finally into the purple of evening.

As the sunlight vanished, the wind blew up, rough and raucous, bringing a pattering of rain against the windows, which slowly strengthened into a heavy shower. And then it poured, the rain rattling the windows and thundering on the roof. The path to the folly would be turning to mud now, and water would be sluicing over the folly itself, chilling the marble, washing it clean. Julia shivered.

She stayed where she was, unable to will her muscles to function, until eventually the rain ended, too, and the world was quiet and dark again.

How much time had passed since she'd come up here? How many hours?

Was Holsworth gone from Grantleigh Hall by now?

She didn't hear him come, or go, but he wouldn't really have dared to stay, would he? Not after that awful scene up on the hill. Not after she'd told him he must go. Surely he'd left without her hearing, under cover of the storm.

She closed her eyes, burrowed her face into the softness of her bedcoverings.

Just when she thought she might actually drift off into sleep, though, a quiet tapping sounded at her door. A jolt went through her—he wasn't still here, was he? He wasn't going to try to talk to her again?

But the voice she heard through the door was a woman's. "Julia?" It was Eleanor. "Julia, please, may I come in?"

It was almost too exhausting to sit up and take the few steps to the door. But she could hardly leave an elderly woman standing out there in the hall.

Eleanor's face, lit by the candle she was carrying, was etched with compassion and worry. "What on earth is going on, child? You've been holed up here forever. Everyone else has had their supper and gone to bed." Not stopping to ask permission, Eleanor bustled about, finding the oil lamp on the side table by the door and using her own candle to light it.

"In-including Major Holsworth?"

"No, dear. I have not seen Holsworth since this morning, but his valet came in mid-morning to pack his bags and go, without a word of explanation to anyone." Her tone suggested a question, but she did not ask it outright.

Julia walked numbly back to stand beside her bed. "Back to India, I suppose."

"India? No, he's not returning there." Julia must have looked shocked, because Eleanor hurried to add, "Didn't he tell you? He gave word to the General before he left that he plans to resign his commission. He's come home to Devonshire for good."

Julia's limbs instantly froze. "He *what*?"

"He's already made arrangements to purchase Clement House—that lovely place along the river Lord Barrow's wanted to sell for a decade now."

"But that's—scarcely five miles from here!" Her pulse went thready, and she had to sink down onto the edge of her bed before she slumped to the floor. It hadn't occurred to her that Holsworth hadn't planned to return to India.

Good Lord—he'd *known* they were going to be neighbors when he went into the hothouse room with her last night, when he'd allowed her to seduce him. He'd known they'd see a great deal of one another from here on in, that they couldn't possibly avoid it in the very small society of the local families.

I've always loved you, Julia.

Her vision faded to near black—she didn't realize Eleanor had moved until she felt the mattress dip beside her, and Eleanor's arm slip comfortingly around her waist.

"What is it, dear?" said the older woman kindly. "Does that news upset you?"

Julia caught her breath. It would do no one any good for Eleanor to realize just how upset she truly was, or why. "It— it surprises me, Aunt," she said. "How could Holsworth possibly afford to purchase such a place?"

"He's become a wealthy man, child, in his own right.

He's won a great deal of prize money in the wars—and rich rewards from Indian princes and nobles grateful for defense against Pindari raids. Besides, he will almost surely have a knighthood at the very least before the year is out, if not a better title than that. He needs a proper English home."

He will live in Devon again. He will be near me.

Her heartbeat throbbed in her throat, down the length of her arms and legs, and up through the curve of her skull. Her body was traitorous, warming despite everything at the thought of Holsworth's nearness, remembering the solid weight of him against her flesh. *But that can never be. That can never be again.*

Julia squeezed shut her eyes, trying to regain her composure. "Well, I suppose he will be happy," she said, forcing the words, "back in the part of the world where he was born."

"Oh, please! Don't give me platitudes, girl!" Eleanor made a harrumphing noise. "You certainly don't have to be polite with me. Something happened, didn't it, between the two of you, when you went walking today? Marcus had all his belongings rushed out of Grantleigh Hall without so much as a fare-thee-well to any of the family, and you've been locked up here ever since, looking as pale as your sheets. Did the two of you...argue?"

Julia's throat closed. Awful tears were rising, and she fought them down as best she could. "You might say that."

"For pity's sake, Julia. What about?"

She couldn't bear to hold it all in anymore. If anyone could see the full complexities of the situation, it was Aunt Eleanor. And Eleanor, at least, would not be likely to pass judgment on anyone else's behavior. Julia lifted her chin and looked Eleanor square in the eye. "Have you had much contact with George Brayles in India?"

"Ah," said Eleanor, with a knowing look. "Marcus told you of his suspicions."

"Then he must have told you, too." Her breathing quickened. "Do you—do you think Brayles could have...turned against king and country?"

"To be honest, I don't know, dear. George Brayles always seemed a rather spineless sort to me. But a traitor? That's harder to say. I had almost no contact with him in Calcutta."

"No?" Julia's heart fell.

"I had a visit or two from his sister when she first arrived, but she was none too keen to visit again when she learned I spent time in the library of Mr. Maji's aunt. *Consorting with the natives*, as her sort would say. Once Miss Brayles learns of my marriage, I've no doubt she'll give me the cut direct should we ever meet again. I don't consider it a loss, frankly. I'd just as soon not have to listen to her natter on about the latest Devonshire gossip from her sister-in-law's letters." Eleanor rolled her eyes. "Dreadful boring stuff."

"But *Mr.* Brayles?"

"As much a snob as the sister, I'm sure. I'm sorry I can't tell you more. Englishmen get up to strange entanglements in India, that's all I can say—things they wouldn't necessarily do at home. And Marcus has a keen eye for all the goings-on. He's a hard man to fool."

Julia's hands twisted anxiously in the fabric of her skirts. What if she'd been wrong? What if Holsworth judged George Brayles rightly, and Christopher was wrong, and everything Holsworth said about the man was true?

She swallowed hard. Could it be possible? She'd been so upset when he suggested the idea to her, so horribly shocked, she'd just wanted to make the whole business go away. Her brain ached now, as though several pairs of hands had plunged inside and were squeezing hard, pulling in different directions.

She turned to Eleanor more urgently. "And those other

Englishmen?" she asked. "What is their opinion of Major Holsworth?"

"Oh, now that's a complicated question, to be sure. His enlisted men would die for him, without a doubt. He's more than earned their loyalty. All men of intelligence respect him greatly, both British and Indian. Unfortunately, not all British officers fall into the category of men of intelligence. A few treated him quite badly."

"And he resented that?"

"Who wouldn't resent that? To be so very capable, and to be questioned and harassed by men of far less talent? I'd have chewed through my sword-belt in frustration. If you ask me, Marcus has always shown far more patience and forbearance than any man should be asked to muster."

Patience and forbearance? Or just the opposite, in the end?

"Oh, I don't know what to believe." Julia's voice broke, and her tears rose so fast, there was no stopping them from spilling onto her cheeks.

"Julia!" cried Eleanor in surprise, turning to embrace her. "Oh, poor child!" She pulled Julia close, her gardenia powder a soft cloud of comfort, and patted her back with a surprising degree of motherly warmth. "Poor dear. My poor, darling girl. This isn't just about Brayles, is it?"

Julia dug in her pocket for a handkerchief, and dabbed it across her face. "Yes, it is," she said, sniffling. "It's all about Brayles."

"No, dear. I mean, Marcus *told* you, didn't he? He's let you know at last."

"Told me what?"

Gently, Eleanor set Julia a bit more upright so she could look her in the eye again. One hand stroked a loosened lock of Julia's hair back behind her ear. The other squeezed Julia's hands in what felt like encouragement. "He told you about his feelings for you. Didn't he?"

Julia's handkerchief dropped from numb fingers. "He— his feelings? Good Lord, he told *you* about that?" Hot embarrassment steamed its way from the top of her head down to her knees. This was Christopher's *aunt* sitting here, apparently well aware of Holsworth's desires. And also maybe… but, no, *surely* he hadn't told Lady Eleanor what happened in the hothouse room. Even Holsworth had more self-control than that.

"Oh, no darling," said Eleanor. "He never said a word. But I've known him a very long time, since he was a boy. He may conceal his more tender feelings from most people, but he can't hide them from me. I watched him at your wedding, and back in India, whenever I read aloud the letters you sent me, I watched his face. He was happy for Christopher, I know he was, and he respected the bond between you. He wouldn't have let you know of his feelings for all the world, not while Chris was alive. But he yearned for you, always."

"But he *shouldn't* have!" she cried. "It's—its *wicked*!"

"Oh, come, my dear. Who amongst us can control what the heart feels? It would only have been wicked had he tried to woo you away from your husband. And far from doing that, he put *oceans* between you, and never breathed his secret to anyone. He's a good man."

"Is he?"

"*Yes*," said Eleanor firmly, giving Julia's knee a pat. "There's no better man on this earth."

On this earth. Fresh tears skimmed down Julia's cheeks, and a surge of emotion nearly choked her—fear mixed with hope, shame and grief with a rising swell of need. "But how can he love me? He scarcely knows me!"

Eleanor chuckled. "How long did it take Christopher to come to love you? An afternoon?"

"That's different!"

"Is it? The two of them were so alike, in so many ways,

despite how dissimilar they looked on the surface. They were true brothers of the heart, if not of the flesh. Is it so surprising they would be drawn to the same woman?"

Julia could scarcely breathe. Could it be true, what Eleanor said? Eleanor didn't seem shocked in the slightest by the idea that Holsworth might love her just as Christopher had.

Then again, Eleanor didn't exactly see the world as other English ladies did.

Nothing shocked Eleanor.

Still, Julia's body felt weightless, floating upwards—all except for the golden bracelet around her wrist. That felt solid, and real, reassuring, a sort of anchor keeping her from drifting away. Her free hand reached for it again, her fingers spreading out along the smooth, curved surface. It felt warm, as always, to her touch.

Eleanor gave her back another pat. "Tell me, Julia—am I wrong about his behavior toward you? Did you know of his feelings before today? Did Marcus ever give you the least sign of passion? While Christopher was alive, did Marcus flatter you? Engage in flirtations with you? Proposition you?"

"No! Of course not! Never. He—I thought he disliked me, in fact."

"There! Isn't that the sign of an honorable man? A man who loved unselfishly, wanting nothing in return? A man who would never so much as let his suffering show? Listen to me, Julia, I watched you, too, this morning—very carefully. When I first arrived in the breakfast room, and when Mr. Maji told you the story of Bharati. And I think perhaps you might not be as indifferent to Holsworth as you might have the world believe."

Julia startled, felt the weight slam back into her body. "Aunt!"

"And why should you be indifferent, dear? Marcus is a

remarkable man. A most a*ttractive* man. Christopher Grantleigh isn't an easy act to follow, I'll admit that—but Christopher would not wish you to spend the rest of your life alone. Nor would he have you marry some other man who is his inferior. Marcus Holsworth is *not* Christopher's inferior, not in anything but the rank of his birth. In every other way, Marcus is Christopher's equal. Possibly more."

Julia jumped to her feet, alarm vibrating through her chest. It was one thing to consider that Holsworth's passion for her might not be dishonorable, but to consider *abandoning* Christopher, to give her loyalties and love to another man—well, that was an another thing entirely. The rules and restrictions of a lifetime bore down on her heart with inexorable force. "This isn't an appropriate thing to discuss!" she cried. "I—I can't. It's impossible."

Eleanor rose, too, with a heavy sigh, and took a few quiet steps about the room. "In what way is it impossible? You are widowed, he is unmarried. The world may judge you for making such a marriage, but the world knows very little about happiness. Dear girl, I may not be a model for proper behavior, but I am most certainly a model for knowing how to be happy. You've lived through terrible pain in the last two years, I know. But happiness is once again within your reach."

"It isn't! Christopher was my life, my soul. I owe him—"

"What? Being miserable for the rest of your existence? How does that honor him?" Eleanor strode over to Julia's dressing table, where all her gifts from Christopher were arrayed—the teak tray, the picture frame, the little carved bowls—and lifted the rosewood hairbrush, idly, or so it seemed. "Look at all these lovely things," she said. "It's like a shrine, but all the treasure made of wood."

"Christopher gave all those to me," said Julia, hurrying over and plucking the hairbrush out of Eleanor's hand. She held it to her chest. "They're precious to me. Beyond precious."

"Because Christopher chose them so well? Knew just what you would like? Treasures of value not because they're made of jewels or precious metal, but because they are carefully, beautifully crafted by human hands?"

"Yes. Precisely. That's the sort of man he was, and he knew I would adore these things."

Eleanor gave her a rueful smile. "Did it ever occur to you *how* Christopher came by those things? How exactly he chose them for you?"

"I don't know. He always had one ready for my birthday —just after Parliament closed for the summer. Many London shops sell imports from India."

"Oh, child. Let me tell you something. I *recognize* every item here. Every single one. I saw them all before—in Calcutta."

Julia's brow furrowed. "Did—did *you* purchase them there? Did Christopher ask you to?"

"Not me, darling," said Eleanor, shaking her head. "*Marcus.* Christopher asked *Marcus* to find you treasures, and ship them home for him."

"*Marcus?*" Julia gasped. "How—how do you know that?"

"I'd go with him to the bazaars, and watch him hunt for hours. He rejected all sorts of geegaws and fancier things, things other Englishmen went wild for. Marcus searched each time until he found the one perfect thing. Something he knew you would love."

Oh. Julia couldn't speak. Her fingers trembled as she turned the hairbrush over in her hands. All these years, she'd held this, brushed her curls out night after night, thinking of Christopher's love for her, thinking this was proof.

But Christopher did *love me. He* did *know me, down to the deepest core of my heart.*

She laid the hairbrush down, gently, and the bracelet bumped gently against its handle.

Oh, the world was more complicated than she had ever imagined.

Much more complicated.

Even breathing in and out suddenly seemed very strange.

"Hear me, Julia," said Eleanor. "If you feel nothing for Marcus, that's one thing. Send him away if you can't love him, can't love with all your heart and soul. But if you think you could have feelings for him, if there's any chance you could love him as truly as you loved my nephew—well, then, life is long, my child. It should not be spent alone."

Julia stared down at the familiar array on her dressing table, all of it suddenly shifted into something unknown, unfamiliar, and the only coherent thought she could manage was the picture of Marcus Holsworth's hands—those strong hands, those gentle hands—sorting through heaps of gold and silver stacked on the tables of some faraway bazaar, and finding *these*, choosing *these*.

For me.

Eleanor bent close and pressed a kiss to Julia's temple. "One thing more, dear girl," she said, "and then I'll leave you in peace. It's another of Bharati's poems. Will you let me recite it to you?"

Julia nodded numbly. She might as well.

"Good," said Eleanor. "This one comes from early in her story, when she was newly fallen in love with that unsuitable young man, and told she couldn't marry him. She was still trying to be a dutiful daughter—doing as her father demanded and staying away from the man who held her heart. But when night came on, she yearned for him, wished she could get a message to him, and call him close to her once more. She describes herself like this:

I stand on the balcony of my father's house,

Begging the wind to carry my voice to my beloved.
I offer my necklaces as a bribe,
My most costly rubies,
But the wind cares nothing for riches,
And it has no pity for a heartsick girl."

HEARTSICK? Julia's own heart gave a throb. The storm winds outside sounded suddenly more harsh and unforgiving than they had before, and she felt terribly empty inside. "Bharati's story doesn't end happily, Aunt. You told me so yourself."

"No, it didn't end happily. Not for her." Eleanor touched a finger to the rim of the bracelet, and gave it a meaningful tap. "But she herself held out hope that others might do better."

Julia stared down at the circlet of gold about her wrist, at its rich gleam in the lamplight, warm as the temptation it represented. And her whole body shook. "That's—that's a fable, Aunt. A fairy tale. I don't—I *can't* believe in that."

Aunt Eleanor sighed, but she said nothing. She gave Julia's arm one last, quick squeeze, and turned to go.

But before she reached the door, a circle of lantern-light came bobbing up from the direction of the staircase, and Julia's maid Peggy came rushing into the room.

"I beg your pardon, ma'am," Peggy said, dropping a quick curtsy, clearly short of breath. "But the footman says we've got visitors. He says it's most urgent that you come down straightaway."

Visitors? At this time of night?

Julia and Eleanor exchanged a glance. But there was nothing else for it—they hurried down the stairs with the maid.

And, indeed, a small group of travelers was gathered in

the foyer, a man, a woman, and two children, all bundled in wool cloaks, looking decidedly rain-soaked and windblown.

Julia's eyes seemed scarcely able to focus on the man—on his familiar face, and the familiar auburn color of the hair peaking out beneath his beaver hat.

But try as she might to blink the sight of him away, she could not escape the simple fact: the man standing just inside the front door of her home was no stranger to her.

He was George Brayles.

CHAPTER 11

George Brayles, here at Grantleigh.

Good God—when would life stop feeling like a dream she'd somehow blundered into while awake?

She wasn't aware she'd stopped dead midway down the stairs until Eleanor's hand at the small of her back gave her a nudge. Anxiety prickled through her, but it would do no good to let it show. Holsworth might be right about this man, but he just as likely might be wrong.

Brayles hardly *looked* threatening. What sort of murderer came straight to the front door, all bedraggled, dripping wet, with mud on his boots and a leaf stuck to his hat, and his little daughter asleep in his arms?

Right beside him stood his sister Abigail, a proper gentle-woman if ever Julia had known one, wrapped in a cloak of fine green wool with a well-trimmed bonnet on her head. Clutching her hand was the older daughter—*Georgina*, that was her name—a rose-cheeked girl of about eight years old, her face still as sweet as it had been in infancy.

Certainly, none of the females seemed a likely candidate for the role of evil co-conspirator.

Good gracious, Julia was in her own home, surrounded by a veritable army of servants. And she was an English-woman, not some sniveling coward. The role of gracious hostess was ingrained in her down to the bone, so she let that carry her forward, as she offered a smile and an outstretched hand.

"Mr. Brayles, Miss Brayles," she said, drawing the woman and young Georgina into quick embraces. "You are home from India! Has there been some trouble? What brings you to Grantleigh at this hour?"

Mr. Brayles, as it turned out, wasn't even paying atten-tion to her. He was staring up the steps at Eleanor, appar-ently disconcerted to see a woman who should be in Calcutta standing on a staircase in Devonshire. "Lady Eleanor!" he exclaimed, and then seemed to have nothing more interesting to add.

Lord—not exactly a clever man.

His sister answered for him. "Lady Grantleigh," she said. "We do beg your pardon. We've just come from London, and I'm afraid our carriage cracked an axle half a mile from here. The storm blew a branch down, right in our path, and when our coachman tried to avoid it, we went into a ditch."

"Oh, dear!"

"Edgerton Park's too far on foot, with the wind so high and more rain on the way. George sent one of the footmen ahead on a horse to let them know of our troubles, and that we've sought shelter here. If you don't mind having us."

For a moment, Julia thought of offering a Grantleigh carriage to take them the rest of the way home, but the chil-dren were clearly at the point of exhaustion. The stable hands and coachmen were all asleep by now, and till they were roused and dressed, the horses harnessed, and the journey made over roads that could prove treacherous in the wet and dark, it would be well past midnight, at the very least.

No decent woman could make the suggestion.

"Of course I don't mind! You are very welcome," Julia said. "You must be terribly chilled, and famished." She turned quickly to Peggy, whispering instructions to wake the housekeeper so she could direct servants to ready rooms and bring something warm to eat.

Eleanor led the way into the parlor. "I'm afraid it will just be Lady Grantleigh and I to entertain you," she said. "The rest of the family has gone to bed."

"You are too kind, truly," said Miss Brayles, blushing a little. "I'm sorry to keep even the two of you from your beds."

Julia paused. Perhaps it would be wise to wake at least Mr. Maji, to have a gentleman aware of what was going on. But, given Eleanor's claims about the Brayles' attitudes towards 'natives,' it might only create more difficulties.

She sighed, and walked into the parlor herself.

Within minutes, the room was abuzz with activity, as housemaids swarmed in to light the lamps and build up the fire in the hearth. The Brayles family all sat down, looking quite relieved, unbundling themselves from their wet cloaks and handing them over to the footmen. Georgina curled up sleepily against her aunt, and the littlest one—*Kate*, that was it—now on her father's lap, relapsed into slumber.

Eleanor observed them all quite regally from her armchair. "Forgive our surprise at seeing you," she said, addressing Mr. Brayles. "I had no idea you were leaving India."

"We did not know you were leaving, either, Lady Eleanor," Brayles replied. "But Calcutta's been full of commotion in the past few months, since the war ended. Everyone's careening about like a table full of billiard balls." He chuckled at his own witticism.

Julia sighed. Brayles seemed so perfectly ordinary.

Conventional, and rather dull. Were there subtle signs of treachery she was missing, in his face, in his voice, in the movements of his hands? How on earth was one to tell?

It did seem odd that they'd arrive like this, purely by chance, so soon after Holsworth's warning. And yet, how could one arrange for a carriage to break down? Surely Brayles hadn't manufactured the sudden storm, or the mud that clung to all their boots.

Despite everything, despite all her doubts, an urgent wish for Holsworth seized her. If nothing else, she knew he never intended to hurt her, and his strong, steady presence beside her would certainly have made her feel safe.

She glanced over at Eleanor. Was she, too, wondering if Brayles had come deliberately, in hopes of destroying the records of his debts?

Whatever she might be thinking, Eleanor seemed quite at her ease, settling in for a neighborly chat. "There's so much new opportunity in Calcutta, though, don't you think, Mr. Brayles?" she said. "No doubt a new wave of British citizens will soon make the journey there, to take advantage of it. I should have thought you'd choose to stay."

Brayles smiled again, this time a little sadly. "True, India will be bursting at the seams with opportunity. But the climate is too hard for the girls, I'm afraid, and in any case, it's time for a change. We don't even plan to stay long at Edgerton Park—such a sad place for me, since I lost Caroline. My elder brother Charles—you will remember him, I think, Lady Eleanor—has invited us to join him in the city of New York, where he plays a diplomatic role. We've made a decent peace with that nation now, too, and Charles thinks he may have some respectable occupation for me."

"New York?" exclaimed Eleanor, laying a hand to her heart. "Such a godforsaken place!"

Brayles actually laughed. "So says a lady who has lived several years in Calcutta!"

Now Eleanor looked truly affronted. She drew herself up straight and skewered Brayles with a glare. "If you had ever joined the Asiatick Society, Mr. Brayles, you would know West Bengal has been a center of literary culture for millennia. Why, the manuscripts held at the Kalighat Temple alone would—"

"Aunt," said Julia delicately. "Perhaps now is not the time to debate the merits of the world's great cities."

Eleanor glared at Julia now, bristling as if she could not imagine a time when one should not leap to the defense of her adopted home. But she quieted.

"I'm sure you are right," said Brayles, in a tone of conciliation. "But New York will be better for my family, I think, than Calcutta was."

At that moment, two more maids came in, bearing trays of biscuits and warmed beef and toasted cheese, as well as a cheerily steaming teapot. Even the children woke for that. They all seemed ravenous—as well they would be after walking a distance on a stormy night.

Julia calmed herself with the little rituals of pouring and serving, and everyone ate in relative quiet—Julia, too, as her suddenly rumbling stomach reminded her she'd had nothing all day but a bit of breakfast toast and tea.

Another interruption followed in the midst of their repast—four of Brayles' servants arrived, muddy up to the knees, huffing and puffing as they lugged a sizeable traveling trunk and several small valises.

"Oh," said Brayles, shooting Julia an apologetic look, as the trunk was heaved into the parlor. "I hope you don't mind that I had them bring our baggage here. I didn't want it left unguarded by the side of the road."

"Perfectly understandable," she said, though she eyed the

trunk with a certain degree of worry. Brayles had arrived quite obviously unarmed, but any number of weapons might be concealed in such a thing.

Abigail Brayles, however, set her plate and teacup on the side table, and patted her mouth with a napkin. She went to the trunk and kneeled before it, undoing the lock. "Forgive me if I find nightclothes for the girls, Lady Grantleigh. They must be put to bed the moment the rooms are ready."

As the lid was lifted, Julia could see the trunk was full of a lady's things, and a very wealthy lady's things at that— costly fabrics and silken shawls, and little parcels of embroidered satin of the sort used to hold necklaces and hair ornaments. Miss Brayles had to dig rather deep to get what she wanted, displacing layers of woolens and stockings and fine lawn petticoats, until she pulled out a pair of child-sized linen night-rails and little lace-trimmed mob caps.

Holsworth had been correct that the family had come into money.

But nothing in the trunk looked the least bit dangerous. Except perhaps to other ladies whose wardrobes would have to compete with such finery.

Brayles, meanwhile, sipped comfortably at his own tea, shifting his weight so little Kate, who'd quickly gobbled down her fill of toasted cheese, could nestle back to sleep on his lap, her thumb tucked firmly into her mouth.

Whatever else the man was, he seemed a doting father.

He heaved a contented sigh, patting his small daughter's back. "It is good to be back in England," he said softly, "if only for a short time. Calcutta was a hard place for us."

"Why is that?" asked Julia, hoping at last she might learn something definitive.

Looking down at his child, Brayles brushed back a copper-colored braid that had drooped across her face. "Kate here had the worst of it. The heat and food did not agree with her. You can see how small she is for her six years." His brow creased, and he stroked his fingers tenderly over the child's cheek. "There were weeks at a time when she'd be seized by awful fevers during the night."

The older daughter, Georgina, whose attention had been absorbed by Cook's famous raspberry-preserve biscuits, chimed in abruptly. "She'd cry and cry! And say she saw birds flying about the room! Big, ugly birds with black shining eyes that watched and watched us! I could never fall back to sleep afterward."

"It was delirium," said Abigail Brayles gently, handing the girl another biscuit and resuming her own seat with the nightclothes in her lap. "We persuaded a Company doctor to see her, but we couldn't afford to pay him much, and he stopped coming." Her voice dropped to little more than a whisper. "Finally, to get the money to bring him back, George had to pawn the family signet ring. It was the most awful time."

The ring. Julia's breath caught in her throat.

Brayles himself heaved a sigh now, and looked at Eleanor with a rueful expression. "Since you are here, Lady Eleanor, I suppose I must say a little more. No doubt you heard some stories about me at that time—some less than savory tales?"

Eleanor's eyes flew wide, but even she was too much the British lady to confirm what he said. She merely regarded him, allowing him to say more.

"My brother had sent me out to Calcutta with perhaps an excess of optimism about how easy it would be for me to make my way there," Brayles continued. "He did not mean to starve us, but the funds we had to hand ran out quickly. I sent letters home, but of course it can be months before a reply comes. In the meantime, in my desperation over my daughter's health, I confess I began to frequent establishments that featured gaming. There was no society of gentleman there to assist me, and I had no other hope of acquiring ready cash. It was necessary to go where the soldiers went—distressingly rough places, I'm afraid. I thought with my superior education I might fare well against them, but…"

"You did not fare well," said Eleanor.

"No." He shook his head, looking humbled. "And the day when I was forced to pawn my ring—that was the very worst of my life." He held up his hand, flashing the ruby at them. "This ring has been passed down in my family since the time of—"

"Queen Elizabeth," finished Eleanor dryly.

Brayles nodded, apparently unconscious of any irony on Eleanor's part. "Thank God," he said, "within that very week, correspondence arrived from my brother, with a more generous influx of funds. And not long after that, we had still more excellent news. By happy chance, a business investment my brother made on my behalf—a small silver mine in the hills—hit a rich vein of ore, and we were well and truly saved from our woes. I was able to pay off the debts I owed, and bring in an excellent physician for Kate, far better than the first. My girl recovered, thank heaven. But even now, when she sleeps, her breathing is not quite right…"

Julia listened closely, and she could indeed hear a slight rasp from the child's lungs. And the girl was certainly on the small side, nowhere near as robust-looking as her older sister.

The story made perfect sense—more or less what Julia herself had surmised when Holsworth first told her his version of the tale—and unless Brayles and his sister were consummate actors, their distress over their circumstances seemed quite sincere. The little girls, certainly, were too young to be lying about the fevers and the delirious dreams of black-eyed birds.

Brayles looked at Eleanor again, a look of chagrin on his

face. "I suppose, Lady Eleanor, Major Holsworth told you what *he* inferred about my conduct during this time."

This time, Eleanor did not make a ladylike demurral. "I will admit he did."

Brayles look dreadfully pained. "Holsworth mistrusted me. Or rather, he inquired into my private business, and misinterpreted what he saw. I admit that the man to whom I pawned my ring was of bad character, very bad character indeed. But that one exchange was the extent of my business with him, I swear. I'd thought because he was English…but never mind that. The moment I learned what sort of treachery he was involved in, I would have redeemed my ring with my own heart's blood, had that been required."

"Holsworth mistrusted you?" prompted Eleanor. "Why was that?"

"He was never inclined to like me." Brayles mouth quirked uncomfortably. "I'm afraid I was unkind to him as a boy. You know the sorts of mischief boys get into, when they are thoughtless and young. But you must believe me—I caused him no difficulties as a grown man. He served king and country well in India, and I respected that. In fact, I made him some overtures of friendship when I first arrived in Calcutta, but he rebuffed me. And when Kate's troubles started…well, I do not like to attribute motives to another man, but he shared his suspicions about me with other officers and gentlemen, even with your late husband, Lady Grantleigh, which meant my brother heard of them as well." He blew out a hard breath. "Holsworth made things rather hot for me in Calcutta, for a while."

A leaden ball seemed to have settled in Julia's stomach. She was less sure than ever what to believe.

Brayles leaned back against the cushions of his chair, his face weary. "My brother can confirm the truth of my story, my lady. I know he made the actual facts known to your husband, when they spoke."

Oh. Holsworth had said nothing about communication between Christopher and Lord Edgerton. Surely Christopher would have informed Holsworth, if he learned Edgerton was the actual source of Brayles' renewed wealth. Holsworth had stormed out the night of their argument, but Christopher certainly would have sent a letter to India informing him of the facts once he had a chance to speak with the viscount. Wouldn't he?

Or had their quarreling prevented it?

Or had a letter been sent, but lost on its long travel across the ocean?

Blast it all. Was Brayles lying to her now? Or had Holsworth indeed misjudged him?

The moment she was out of earshot of Brayles, she'd send a footman of her own hurrying to Edgerton Park to ask the viscount for his side of the tale. But even if her man made good time on the dark roads, it would be nearly dawn before she could expect a reply.

Now Brayles shook his head meditatively. "It's a strange place, India, that's all I can say. A very strange episode in my life. I am so very glad to be done with it."

Before Julia managed to form a coherent response, Mrs. Collins, the housekeeper, appeared at the parlor door, looking expectant. "Ma'am," she said. "The bedrooms have all been readied."

Abigail Brayles did not hesitate. "If you will excuse us, Lady Grantleigh," she said, rising gratefully to her feet, "Georgina looks about to sink through the cushions."

Her skull aching, Julia rose as well. Nothing more would be learned tonight.

With the briefest of farewells, the Brayles went off to their chambers, and Julia went up to her own, pausing only to scrawl a quick message to Brayles' brother the viscount and send her most trusted footman on the fastest horse to Edgerton Park.

After that, exhausted as she was, she could barely make logical replies to Peggy's chatter as the maid helped her out of her dress and took down her hair. Her only clear thought was of the comforting solace of her bed.

Though when Peggy left, Julia did take a moment to securely lock her door. And to wedge a heavy chair against it.

Just in case.

She crawled beneath the counterpane, expecting to drop off to instant oblivion. But sleep did not come easily. The bracelet seemed to push against her wrist, no matter how she turned on her pillow, and she couldn't find a position in which her arm felt comfortable.

And somehow, every time her mind did begin to drift, she found herself awakened by the strangest, most unsettling sensation that Holsworth was in the room with her.

And that his hand was holding hers.

CHAPTER 12

*S*omething bumped in the darkness.

Julia sat up in bed, confused, trying to will herself back to consciousness. She must have fallen asleep after all, and now a noise had woken her.

She strained to hear the sound again, but the house was utterly quiet. And yet she felt a disconcerting sense of commotion, of some wild activity going on somewhere not far away.

There! The noise again. Goodness, it was *tapping*—someone just outside her room. A faint sheen of candlelight gleamed through the crack beneath the door.

And then there was a voice. "Lady Grantleigh?"

Whose voice? A woman's, but not Peggy's, and not either of Christopher's aunts.

Julia rubbed at her eyes. There was something important she was supposed to remember.

"*Please*, Lady Grantleigh," said the voice again, more urgently—and that snapped Julia to full alertness. Of course —the visitors who'd arrived. It was Abigail Brayles at her door.

"What is it?" she called.

"It's little Kate," said Miss Brayles, sounding quite relieved to get an answer. "She's not well."

Stumbling slightly, Julia felt for her robe on her bedside chair and nudged her feet into her slippers. For just a moment, she considered not unlocking her door at all, but the woman sounded so worried. And the child's lungs *had* been rasping audibly before they went to bed.

So she unwedged the heavy chair, undid the lock, opened the door. Miss Brayles stood there in her nightdress, holding a candle, looking terribly pale. "Our walk through the damp night air was too much for her," the woman said, her voice full of alarm. "Her breathing's gone all rough again, and I fear fever will set in soon if we don't send for a physician."

"Oh," said Julia. "Let me wake Lady Lambert and—"

"I tried! She wouldn't answer. She must be deep asleep." The candlestick trembled in Miss Brayles' hands, and her eyes looked a little wild. "If you could send a footman for the doctor? Please—Doctor Mills, does he still have his practice? He was always so good and kind when Caroline was ill."

It seemed beyond churlish to resist her pleas. "Dr. Mills," Julia said, fastening the tie of her robe. "Yes, he's not far from here. All right. Of course."

"Thank you, my lady." Miss Brayles seized her hand and hurried with her down the stairs, the candlelight streaking the walls with bands of light and shadow. "George is walking with Kate downstairs, to keep her upright, trying to clear her lungs."

Indeed, once they reached the foyer, Julia could hear the faint sounds of someone moving nearby.

"Over here," said Miss Brayles, tugging her along.

Julia thought perhaps they were heading to the parlor, but Miss Brayles pulled her further down the hallway. Still muddled with sleep, her brain didn't fully register until the last moment that Miss Brayles was leading her into Christopher's study.

Miss Brayles pushed the door open.

Oddly, every oil lamp in the room was brightly lit.

And George Brayles was standing there. Leaning forward over Christopher's desk. His hands gripping a sheaf of papers.

And there was no sign of the child.

Julia's heart lurched. *Oh, no. No.*

Cold fear washed through her belly. She glanced around —the desk drawers and the cabinets were open. The shelves had been ransacked, with all the steward's account-books and ledgers strewn across the desk and floor.

Dear God. He'd been searching through what he thought were Christopher's things.

She'd been a fool. Such an utter fool.

Everything Holsworth had warned her about must be true.

She glanced towards Abigail Brayles, hoping to see her equally shocked by the scene, but the woman calmly pulled the study door shut, and leaned her body back against it, blocking Julia's retreat.

Brayles straightened now and looked at Julia, his eyes anxious, but not with the tender anxiety of a father with a sick child. "You will tell me please, Lady Grantleigh," he said gruffly, "where those ledgers are. The ledgers Holsworth stole and brought back from India."

Damn it all. Why on earth had she sent Holsworth away? Why in God's name hadn't she believed him?

Despite her trembling limbs, she squared her shoulders as best she could. "I don't know what you're talking about." She forced herself to keep her eyes on the man, not give him any sign her attention was on the study door. Was she strong enough to push Abigail Brayles out of her path before George could come from behind the desk to grab her? If she could just get the heavy door open again, she could scream loud enough that even a dozing footman might hear her. Otherwise, the study walls were too thick for her voice to be heard.

"Oh, spare me!" sneered Brayles. "Your husband was the sort of man who couldn't keep his business from his wife. You do know what I'm talking about. When we spoke earlier tonight, it was perfectly clear you knew."

He lifted the flap of his coat—revealing a leather strap around his chest, with two pistols holstered. He drew one out, undid the safety latch, and pointed it at her.

"Do not call out for anyone, my lady," he said. "If you are quiet, and give me what I want, I give you my word as a gentleman that my family will leave here immediately and not trouble you again."

"A gentleman?" she said, pleased that her voice did not waver. "Not according to Major Holsworth."

"*Holsworth*?" Brayles' tone was ugly. "So your husband did share the major's accusations with you. But what can a man like that understand of a man like me, or what I've faced?" He strode forward, the pistol's engraved barrel aimed straight at her chest. "The humiliation of being sent to India, without enough money in my pocket, with my child ill. If *Holsworth* were a gentleman, he'd have come to my aid. He'd have spoken to me, and *only* me, about what he learned, instead of spreading my shame to anyone who'd listen. A true gentleman does not expose another gentleman's flaws and peccadillos."

Peccadillos? Was that how Brayles viewed what he had done? Betrayal of king and country? Aiding a foreign power in time of war?

She tried to calm her thundering heart, tried to *think*. What options did she have against him now? No weapons lay within reach, and it would hardly help to throw a book at him.

Would he actually shoot her if she tried to run? Did it fall within his definition of a *true gentleman* to murder a lady while he was a guest in her home?

Considering his attitude towards treason, she could only guess it did.

Just one reasonable thought occurred to her—if she could frighten him sufficiently, make him believe he was in danger here, he might flee instead of hurting her. No doubt he was a coward at heart.

She raised her chin and prepared to lie. "He's here at Grantleigh, you know. Holsworth. Watching for you."

Brayles blinked in obvious surprise. "*Holsworth?* Holsworth is in India."

"No," she said. "He arrived with Lady Eleanor last night. It wasn't my husband who told me about the ledgers. Holsworth told me. He was quite sure you'd be coming here. And I know he's well prepared to deal with you."

Brayles stared at her long and hard, and she could almost see the calculations taking place behind his eyes. "You're bluffing," he said at last. "If Holsworth were here, he'd have shown himself by now."

Miss Brayles nodded, too. "She's lying, George," she said. "I can see it on her face."

Julia shut her eyes in frustration, and the wish that Holsworth actually was nearby hit her with a stabbing pain.

But she herself had sent Holsworth away.

What choice was left? Brayles had that second pistol, clearly primed and ready, so he was prepared for considerable violence. How many might die if she *did* manage to call for help? Her mind flashed on the faces of the Grantleigh footmen, nearly all of whom had grown up in the village or on surrounding farms, and she couldn't bear to think of any of them taking a bullet because of her mistakes. She had her duty as the lady of the manor, and it was to protect her household.

She would have to find some way out of this herself.

For the moment, getting Brayles and his weapons out of the manor house was her priority. She wasn't a good liar, but luckily, telling the truth was the quickest way to ensure he left.

"The ledgers are not here," she said, firmly. "We moved all Christopher's private books and papers to the dower house six months ago, so the steward could have this room to conduct estate business until the new earl comes to Grantleigh Hall."

Brayles stared at her again, then nodded, apparently seeing the sincerity in her eyes. "I know the place," he said. "Barely a mile down the river road from here. And you shall accompany me, my lady. No doubt you know the location of the keys which will admit us?"

"In the parlor," she said. "I keep them in my writing desk."

Waving for his sister to follow, Brayles took hold of Julia's upper arm, and shoved her roughly into the hall, propelling her into the parlor with such force, she nearly tripped and fell into the huge traveling trunk that still lay open on the floor.

He skirted her around it, pushing her towards her own dainty desk, which was tucked into a corner near the hearth.

In the edge of her vision, she caught sight of the heavy iron poker propped against the mantle piece. If she could get hold of it, maybe...

But Brayles poked her hard in the ribs with the mouth of the pistol, keeping her too close to the desk to have much chance of reaching for it.

"Hurry," Brayles said. He turned to Abigail. "Sister, get

the girls up as quietly as you can. The carriage awaits us at the end of the drive. Never mind our baggage. Do you hear me, Abigail? We've clothes enough for the sea voyage in the coach, and all our gold and silver. I shall buy you a whole new wardrobe when we get where we're going."

"Yes, George," Miss Brayles said, with a surprising note of irritation in her voice.

"Have the coachman drive out to the main road, to the stand of willows just before Seaton Bridge. If he pulls under cover of the hanging branches, you won't be seen in the darkness. Promise me you'll do just as I say. The dower house isn't far from there. I will not be long."

Miss Brayles nodded then, and slipped from the room, quiet as a wraith.

Even as Julia unlocked the drawer and reached inside it for the ring of dower house keys, she cast an arch look in Brayles' direction. "I thought your carriage had broken down."

"Our coach is waiting for us outside, quite undamaged." Brayles sounded smug. "We never meant to go to Edgerton Park. Ironically, the one man who believed Holsworth's accusations was my own brother, the viscount. He wished to keep it quiet, of course—he couldn't bear the thought of my being arrested. Not for my sake, but for his own. He's the one who ordered me to the new world, where my shame, should it be exposed, could do less harm to the Edgerton title."

Lord Edgerton. Good lord, what time was it? Would the viscount have received the message she sent him by now, telling him of his brother's visit and asking if his brother's claims were true? If he knew what kind of man George Brayles truly was, surely he'd realize she was in danger.

Again, a powerful longing for Holsworth seized her. If only she hadn't sent him away today, *he'd* be here now, he'd protect her now. Her mind filled with the image of his face gazing up at her as he knelt before her in the hothouse room —only yesterday night, though it seemed a hundred years ago—and even now, she felt his tenderness, his kindness, his concern washing over her, wrapping about her like a cloak.

I've always loved you, Julia.

Why had it been so hard for her to let him say that? Why had she reacted with such pride, such ladylike rigidity, regarding it as an assault on her honor?

Good God, everyone kept telling her that Christopher would only want her to be happy, and here she'd thrown away the best chance of happiness she could imagine.

It would have been so easy to love him, too.

"Hurry!" insisted Brayles again, giving her ribs another jab.

"I'm trying!" she said, making a show of digging in the drawer, as if the keys were not exactly in the rear right-hand corner where she always left them.

Brayles clearly thought himself clever, but his intellect seemed none too powerful to her. And he was obviously preoccupied with his many grudges against men he blamed for his struggles. If she just kept talking to him, probing a little at those sore spots, the distraction might use up enough of his brain capacity to give her some small chance to outwit him.

She wiggled her hand about in the drawer, rattling the quills and stubs of sealing wax to make it sound as if the drawer were a disorganized jumble. "So," she remarked as she did so, "you will be a dutiful younger brother, and go to the New World as you are bid?"

Brayles actually chuckled. "Oh, I'll go. But not where I am bid. A boat awaits us at Seaton harbor, to take us to a larger ship. We'll be out of the country before the sun has fully risen, off to Bermuda, maybe, New Orleans, perhaps. I'll decide that as we go. I don't intend to be found."

She blinked up at him innocently. "Then why must you get the ledgers back?"

"My brother may care only about the Edgerton title, but I care about my personal good name as well. Who knows? The current viscount has no son, and two of my older brothers have no children at all. I'm the youngest of us. Perhaps one day, the title will pass to me. If it does, I should like to be free to make my return to England again."

"No doubt," she said, and blundered about in the drawer a few moments more.

"Damn it!" he said, losing patience with her. "The keys!"

All right. That was apparently enough provocation for now. She let her fingers close around the keys and then turned back to Brayles, holding up the jangling ring, hoping he'd be absorbed enough in the sight not to notice she'd left the desk drawer open. Lady Eleanor and the housemaids knew her habits well—if any of them noticed it, they might realize where Brayles was taking her.

It didn't give her much hope, but it was something.

Brayles snatched the keys into his own fist and, to her surprise, looked down at them for one unguarded moment—and that was her chance.

She dove to her right, grabbed the iron poker and then swung it with all her might against Brayles' back.

He went sprawling into her desk, and she tried to dash around him, but he was quicker and stronger than she thought. He righted himself before she was even halfway past him, grabbed her violently by the wrist with one hand and swung his other arm through the air, bringing the butt of the gun down hard between her shoulder blades.

She pitched forward, arms wheeling, and crashed atop the open trunk, bruising one forearm on one edge of the metal rim, and all but cracking her rib cage as she landed full force on one brass-reinforced corner.

Brayles' fist seized her by the back of her robe and hauled her about so she sat on the floor, and he crouched beside her with the barrel of the gun digging into her forehead. She squeezed shut her eyes, sure the smell of sulphur as the gunpowder ignited would be the last sensation she ever had on earth.

"Don't!" hissed Brayles, his voice furious. "Don't try to cross me again!" But he didn't pull the trigger. Instead, he hoisted her to her feet and strong-armed her out the front door onto the drive, now burying the pistol cruelly against her already aching ribs.

They didn't have far to go. Down the drive beyond the boxwood hedge, a tall male servant was waiting, holding a horse harnessed to a small curricle, its lanterns shuttered. Brayles shoved her into the servant's burly arms while he climbed into the driving seat, then signaled for the servant to pass him up to her, as casually as if she were a satchel. "Help Miss Brayles and the girls out from the house," he commanded, the servant, "and be quick about it. No noise."

"You don't want someone to go with you, sir?"

"No. I can handle the lady, and we'll travel faster alone. Just do as you're told, and be sure the coach stays hidden by the Seaton Bridge until I arrive. And *don't* let my sister press you to carry her trunk back out from the parlor. It's played a useful role in our little charade, but now she'll have to sacrifice it. You made a racket like a herd of elephants when you brought it in, and we can't risk that noise again now."

"Yes, sir," the servant said.

And then, with the reins in one hand and the pistol in the other, shoved tight against Julia's side, Brayles urged the horse into motion, and they were riding down the gravel path that led to the river road, which they'd follow to the dower house.

The air was surprisingly brisk for springtime, the wind

high and wet with the scent of the rain, and she shivered in her thin nightclothes. All the leaves of the trees were whipping about, showing their pale undersides, and she supposed another shower might break before they reached their destination.

She had little time to think, or formulate another plan. Brayles knew the lay of the land, and between the moonlight and the glow of the lantern he'd uncovered once they were well out of view of the house, he made good time, even when they left the gravel path and turned on to the muddy road.

The sense of unreality that had gripped her ever since last night returned in full force. Before it seemed possible that they had traveled a mile, they'd arrived at the dower house, and Brayles was steering her inside. The place looked like something from a dream—dark and still, the furnishings all draped in white linen meant to keep off the dust. The breeze followed them through the door, stirring the air, making the white coverings flutter, and the light of Brayles' lantern cast strange deformed shadows on the walls.

This place was to have been her home once the new earl found himself a wife. How drear and drab and lifeless it had seemed. How horrible the prospect was of being walled up here forever.

Though she supposed she would never have to live here now.

Surely, Brayles did not intend to let her live at all.

She hadn't really wanted to admit that to herself until now, but if he had any hope of preserving his good name going forward, he couldn't afford to leave her as a witness to his crimes. He'd admitted his guilt to her, kidnapped her, assaulted her with a weapon. His own brother the viscount might be content to cover up his villainy, but the Countess of Grantleigh could not be expected to do so.

So the Countess of Grantleigh must die.

Dread poured through her. And a terrible, surprising sense of loss.

For so much of the past eighteen months, in her mourning for Christopher, she'd thought often of what it would be like to simply leave this world and follow him. It was not in her nature to do such a thing deliberately, but the prospect hadn't frightened her. She'd imagined it as a relief.

But not anymore. Suddenly, she wanted very much to keep living.

She wanted life.

And she wanted Holsworth. Desperately.

Of course, Brayles didn't care in the slightest what she wanted. "Lord Grantleigh's papers," he insisted. "Where did you put them? Lead me there. And don't try any more tricks."

"The library," she said. Resignedly, she led the way to the back of the modest house, into a room little bigger than her parlor at the Hall. Bookcases lined the walls, their contents, too, draped in protective white linen. But she'd been meticulous in caring for Christopher's books, and she knew exactly where all the notebooks and ledgers had been put.

There was a whole shelf of such things—and she did remember half a dozen that were filled with columns of numbers and unfamiliar names, in handwriting that was neither Christopher's nor his steward's, on paper thicker and more yellow than the familiar British make. When she was packing everything away, she hadn't thought much about them. Christopher had documents and manuscripts of all sorts which made no sense to her.

But these were certainly the ledgers Brayles was looking for.

She pushed aside the linen draping, and pulled the books from the shelf one after the other, her hands shaking.

"Put them on the table there," said Brayles. "And page

through them for me. Show me the start and ending dates." He held up the lantern for light, but stood back warily, keeping the pistol trained on her chest.

She flipped through the pages, pointing out dates and Brayles' name whenever she saw it.

One volume after the other, until she reached the end of the stack.

"Good," he said, satisfied. "That will be all of them." Careful to keep his eye on her, he pulled a linen drape from the nearest chair and tossed it into her arms. "Now bind them all into a bundle with that, and tie it up tightly."

Her mind gone empty of everything but despair, she made quick work of the job, and soon the ledgers were wrapped up as securely as a swaddled baby.

She swallowed against the tension in her throat. "You will keep your word now, as a gentleman?" she asked him, sliding the bundle in his direction. It seemed utterly unlikely that he would, but perhaps his training as a gentleman would kick in if she asked. "You will let me go?"

"Do you doubt me?" said Brayles, sounding genuinely offended. "I wasn't lying, Lady Grantleigh. I will return you to your home, and then be on my way."

She nodded, trying to look as though she believed him. But his coach would be waiting for him by the Seaton Bridge, and Grantleigh Hall was back in the other direction.

He stepped closer, smiling down at her in a courteous manner, and took her chin between the fingers of his free hand, tipping her face up towards his. "You should be glad I'm an honorable man, my dear. Look at the two of us, alone here together, and you as lovely as you ever were." His gaze suddenly narrowed, and heated. "If I weren't an honorable man, I'd have you now, on this tabletop, wouldn't I, and take my pleasure any way I liked. I'm certain I'd enjoy it."

Her eyes widened in horror.

"However," he said, releasing her chin and stepping back. "I won't touch you. I recognize that you are a lady, one whose husband never did any harm to me. In fact, he proved extraordinarily valuable in keeping me out of trouble, didn't he?" Brayles smirked now. "Such a very noble, trusting man he was, Lord Grantleigh."

Blind anger swelled up instantly, irresistibly, and she flew at him without thought, pounding him with her fists. "You bastard! You blackguard! You have no claim to decency, and no right to speak my husband's name!"

Brayles was driven backwards for a moment by the sheer fury of her blows, but he was bigger and stronger than she was, and before she could cause him any real harm, he seized her arm again, rough enough to bruise her, and threw her back against the shelves. The sharp edge of his hip shoved into her belly, trapping her against the boards, and the pistol pressed into her hair.

She closed her eyes again, waiting for the crack of the gun, expecting to be dead in a heartbeat.

But Brayles didn't shoot. He kept her pinned there for several seconds, his breath harsh in her ear, the fingers that squeezed her flesh shaking with his anger. "Hush, girl," he hissed. "That's quite enough. I've been more than decent toward you, but if you attack me again, I'll decide you're not a lady after all."

She let out a sob. What difference did it make?

Fighting back her tears, she tilted her head back as best she could and looked him straight in the eye. "You know if you harm me," she said, keeping her voice low and forceful by pure act of will, "Holsworth will find you. You've never been able to hide from *him*, have you? He swore to my husband that he would protect me, and if you don't let me go, he'll hunt you down, even if it takes until his dying day. Knowing how he deals with his enemies, I doubt it will take him anywhere near that long."

Brayles listened, his jaw slowly dropping. Uncertainty flickered in his eyes. Yes, the thought of Holsworth coming after him did frighten him.

His fingers eased their hold on her arm, though he didn't release her entirely. He pulled her away from the bookcase, and whirled her around to the table again. He thrust his chin at the bundle of ledgers. "You'll carry those," he said, in his sneering voice. "It'll keep your arms busy."

All right. So at least he wasn't going to kill her here. She gathered up the bundle, and he pushed her ahead of him again, back outside, where a drizzle had begun to fall. For a moment, she considered running. But she'd never been very fast, and Brayles' legs were far longer than hers.

And she knew he could do worse things to her than put a bullet quickly through her brain.

Her hoisted her up onto one side of the curricle, the ledgers still in her arms, and then clambered his way back into the driving seat. With a crack of the whip, he brought the horse around, and they headed down the short driveway to the river road again. She closed her eyes, hugging the ledgers to her chest for whatever comfort they could provide, and prayed against all odds that somehow she would get out of this alive.

But the moment they reached the road, Brayles wheeled the curricle to the right, not the left. As she'd predicted, he was heading away from Grantleigh Hall, in the direction of the river road that would lead to Seaton Bridge.

Surely Brayles didn't plan to take her with him all the way to Bermuda or New Orleans or wherever else he planning to go. And he couldn't leave her in Britain, where she'd tell everyone the truth about him.

This length of the river road was dark and wild and little

traveled. It featured an ample supply of ridges and cliffs and drop-offs down into the water, where a body might never be found.

She wanted to weep. *Christopher*, she thought.

Holsworth.

What could she possibly do? Try to leap from the vehicle before Brayles had time to shoot her? Try to bring Brayles rolling down with her, hoping he'd break a limb or his neck without the same happening to her?

She stared off hopelessly into the night, willing some miracle to occur.

The drizzle was thickening now into rain, and they'd reached the narrow part of the road, where thickly-wooded hillside sloped up sharply to the left of them, pockmarked with boulders, and the ground fell off perilously to the right, where anyone who strayed even slightly from the road risked pitching fifty feet down to the river roaring along beneath them.

Brayles' full attention had to stay on controlling the horse, which surely disliked being urged forward so fast on such a treacherous path through darkness and slippery mud, with a double load of riders to pull.

And so she was sure Brayles didn't see the remarkable thing she caught sight of—a flash of something pale in the trees up on the ridge off to their left, a little way above them. Something keeping pace with them, even on terrain far rougher than the road.

It was gone almost as soon as she saw it, vanished behind boulders and branches and leaves. Perhaps she'd only imagined it.

And yet her heart soared with sudden hope.

If someone was there, if Lord Edgerton had received her message, and somehow figured out where his brother had taken her...but that seemed too improbable to be believed.

How could he know the ledgers had been moved to the Grantleigh dower house? Why would he be looking for her on the river road to Seaton, not out on the main thoroughfare?

The hope she'd felt thinned to a desperate thread.

And, yet, if there was any chance, any chance at all that they were being followed, she had to do what she could to help their pursuer keep track of them in the dark.

Brayles still had the lanterns mostly shuttered, and she had no other source of light. But perhaps she could help give away their location with some noise.

The road was worsening as the rain fell, and the horse was slowing regardless of Brayles' impatient urging. If someone was out there, and didn't have to move quite so quickly through all the obstacles on the ridge, they might even be able to get close enough to make out the words.

"Tell me something, Mr. Brayles," she said, using her best social-call enunciation. "Did you know what you were doing, when you were in the pay of the tea-shop man?"

Brayles shot her an incredulous look. "*What?*"

"When you passed on what you heard from military officers of the East India Company, did it occur to you *why* that man wanted to hear such things so much? Enough that he would give you a great deal of money in exchange?"

She risked a quick glance back up the ridge, to see if she could spot that flash of movement again. But she saw nothing. Heard nothing but the rain. *Damn it all.*

"Does it matter?" Brayles answered scornfully, his eyes back on the road.

"It does if those secrets were sold to the Pindari, and English soldiers died as a result."

Brayles' fist tightened visibly on the reins, and the tip of his pistol burrowed harder into her side. "I did what I had to do! What difference could it possibly make which Indian factions were most powerful in India—they're all savages, anyway. No British society will ever be truly secure in such a place. The Indians aren't capable of civilization."

"Lady Eleanor doesn't think so. Major Holsworth doesn't think so." She glanced again up the ridge—*still nothing*. Had she merely imagined the pale flash? "In fact, just yesterday, he reminded me that India had a great intellectual culture a thousand years before Europe stopped burning witches."

"*Holsworth* is a savage," Brayles sneered.

"Holsworth is a man of honor," she said confidently. "He would never sell his integrity for money. And he would never turn traitor. Unlike you, Mr. Brayles."

With a cry of anger, Brayles pulled back hard on the reins, bringing the horse to a skidding stop. "Enough! I've heard all I care to hear from you!"

Please, she thought, as Brayles leapt down from his seat and strode around to her side of the curricle, the pistol constantly trained at her head. *Please let someone be out there.*

"Climb down here!" Brayles commanded. "And bring those ledgers."

"Why should I?"

"Come now," he said, his voice changing to a wheedling tone. "I've already made it quite clear I mean you no harm, but I need your help in destroying the evidence against me. I have only one hand free, after all. I want you to undo that bundle, and throw the ledgers, one at a time, over the edge into the water. That's all." He waved the pistol at her head. "Do as I say, Lady Grantleigh, and all will be well."

Liar. But she had little choice but to do what he said. At least they had stopped now. If anyone was attempting to follow them along that perilous ridge, she could buy a little time. Give them every possible chance to catch up.

She stepped down from the curricle gracefully, slowly, as a proper lady should. The rain had soaked the linen bundle, so of course she had an excuse to tug and pull and struggle for some moments with the tight, wet knot.

"Damn you," said Brayles. "Will you hurry?"

"I am doing my very best, Mr. Brayles," she informed him. There was only so long she could drag out the procedure, though, and at last the edges of the linen parted, and she was obliged to pull the ledgers free.

"Now throw the blasted things," said Brayles. "And get them well into the water."

"It will have to be one at a time," she said, arching a brow at him, "if you want me to manage that. My arms are not strong. Unlike yours, I'm sure."

"Just do it."

She made it last as long as she could manage, swinging each one back and forth a few times to build momentum before she sent it sailing out over the embankment into the racing water. But there were only six ledgers, and before she knew it, she was done.

"Very good," said Brayles. "Thank you for your assistance, my lady."

Trying to keep her calm, she turned to climb back into the curricle, hoping against hope that Brayles would drive her on from here and give her even a few more minutes in which she might have some faint chance of rescue.

But instead he darted forward and seized her around the waist.

Oh, God. And still no one had come.

"Let go of me!" she shouted, as loudly as she could through her terror.

"I will in a moment," he said, shoving her closer to the edge. The fingers of his free hand stabbed into her hair, grabbing a thick hank of it and twisting painfully. The pistol was against her temple.

"For God's sake, Brayles," she pleaded, hot tears

springing to her eyes. "Don't shoot me. I've done nothing to harm you."

"I'm not going to shoot you, my lady. Haven't I promised that?" But he was pushing her forward, beyond the flat edge of the road, onto the little sliver of rough ground that was all that remained before the sudden plunge. "I can't have them find you with a bullet in your head."

She tried to struggle against his grip, but he was too strong. Her feet were sliding forward, through stones and pebbles that bounced off into the open air, clattering down, down, into the terrible darkness.

He yanked her head back cruelly, leaning in to whisper in her ear. "Poor Lady Grantleigh, so overcome with grief. Such a sad story. One evening without her widow's weeds, and she knew there was no more life for her. She rode out into the hills the very next night, and flung herself to a watery death."

Damn him. She tried to scrabble with her feet, find some solid purchase she could use to her advantage, but the ground beneath her was all loose stone or slick mud, and she succeeded only in losing one of her slippers, sending it flying out into the void.

Holsworth had called her *formidable*, though, and she'd be damned if she'd stop fighting to the last. She owed him that, at least. If nothing else, she could clutch at Brayles' coat, try to get enough of a grip on it without him realizing to take him tumbling down with her.

She braced herself for the final push, but still Brayles held her just at the edge, laughing softly in her ear. "Do you wonder, my lady, how I know you only put off your widow's weeds last night?"

"I don't care," Julia bit out. All at once, she remembered the leather holster strap Brayles wore around his chest. His coat was buttoned over it now, but the high-waisted cutaway style might allow her to shove her fingers under the hem and seize the strap at the final moment. Then he'd have nothing more to gloat about, and at least her death would not be entirely in vain.

Brayles, for his part, wasn't deterred by her expressed lack of interest in his explanation. "One of the Grantleigh house-maids has been in my pay for two years now," he said, quite pleased with himself. "A poor farmer's daughter, desperate to better her lot in life, eager for a windfall of gold such as I was able to provide."

"Does that make you clever?" she asked. The strap dipped to its lowest point on the left, she recalled, just below his waist. If she bent back her right hand just beneath the bottom button of his coat, she ought to be able to hook her fingers around the strap before he was able to fully let her go.

"But it's such a satisfying irony, don't you think?" Brayles said, in lieu of answering her question. "The Grantleighs are so fond of welcoming the lowest of the low into their house-holds. How fitting that they should be brought down by one. The girl was an ignorant thing—she didn't know enough to inform me of Holsworth's return, if in fact he did return, and she never could find my ledgers for me—but she did me another fine service. I couldn't have Lord Grantleigh telling anyone else the details of what he'd seen in those ledgers, now could I? His memory was famously excellent, after all. Who knows who might have interpreted things more cyni-cally than he did?"

The mention of Christopher got Julia's attention. "What are you talking about?"

"I'm telling you that this girl, whilst in his lordship's study, took a substance I sent her and slipped it into his lord-ship's brandy, a little at a time. A substance I got from that *tea-shop man*, as you so quaintly call him. A substance very hard to detect, but which did wonders to weaken an already weak heart…"

All other thoughts fled from Julia's mind, and her limbs went limp, cold horror flooding her veins. "Oh, dear God!" she cried. "You mean you *killed* him! You murdered Christopher!"

"I did," said Brayles. And then, his satisfaction apparently complete, his arms tensed violently around her, readying to send her over the edge.

And in that moment, the world seemed to explode.

Blinding light and an ear-rending blast shattered the quiet darkness of the night, and the fresh, rain-washed air was suddenly chokingly thick and impossible to breathe.

The pressure of Brayles' arms dropped away, and Julia fell helplessly downwards.

But onto her knees.

Onto the ground where she'd been standing.

And it was *Brayles* who pitched forward, his legs flaying just inches in front of her, and his arms flung wide. And then she watched him falling, far and fast, down the precipice towards the river, his body spinning once through the air as it plunged, before vanishing into the shadows below.

Julia was stunned, her knees and her palms pressing into the mud and stones there at the edge of the road. She wasn't falling. She was still breathing, her body all in one piece, unbroken. How was it even possible?

Then she heard men's voices, recognized the hovering stink of sulphur, saw an unfamiliar pair of booted legs come out of nowhere to stand where Brayles had been standing only a few seconds before, their owner apparently looking over the edge of the cliff to see just where Brayles had gone. The butt of a rifle swung by his knee.

And even more miraculously, *Holsworth* was suddenly there beside her.

He was kneeling in the very same mud she was, as large and strong and solid as ever, and she could hear his deep, familiar voice murmuring something soft and comforting, and, even through the gunsmoke, she could smell the wonderful scent of his cologne.

How could it be? How could it be?

She'd sent him away, far away.

And she was supposed to be dead.

But he *was* there, and he seemed to be quite sure she was alive, because he was spreading a warm coat over her shoulders. And he was pressing kisses into her hair, and pulling her against his body, and wrapping her tight in his arms.

CHAPTER 13

*M*arcus lifted Julia from the ground, trying to keep as much of her body as possible covered with his coat, and wishing desperately for a woolen blanket. She was soaked to the skin and badly chilled, and quite obviously in shock.

That bastard Brayles had nearly killed her.

Marcus had thought he'd go mad when their path across the ridge was blocked by that sudden huge outcropping of rock, and they'd had to ride far uphill before they found a way around it again.

If they hadn't heard her scream, they might never have located her again in time.

And if Brayles hadn't stepped sideways just before he went to hurl her off the edge, neither Marcus nor Lord Edgerton would have had a clean shot at the man that wouldn't have taken Julia's life as well.

Edgerton was still frozen at the edge of the drop-off, staring down into the gorge.

Hard to blame him. It wasn't every day a man shot his own brother in the back.

Or watched him plummet to his death.

Still, George Brayles hadn't been much to speak of as a brother. And Edgerton wasn't being terribly useful just standing there.

"Edgerton!" Marcus called. "We must get Lady Grantleigh back to Grantleigh Hall. She needs dry clothes and a fire, and possibly a physician as well. So if your horses won't find their way home on their own, tie their leads to the back of the curricle. You must take the reins and drive so I can tend the lady. And give me your damned coat, man. She needs it! Hurry!"

Edgerton had been a military man, too, once. The battle-field tone seemed to penetrate his trance, and he sprang ably into action.

Soon they were moving, Edgerton handling the reins expertly, and Marcus was free to turn his full attention to the woman in his arms.

Julia was very quiet, curled up in his lap, and shivering hard. He arranged the top of Edgeworth's coat carefully over her head to keep her from losing more heat from there, then slipped his own arms beneath his coat so her could rub her back and chafe her arms, and keep her tight against his chest so his body could warm her.

At first he was afraid she'd lost consciousness, but then he became aware her fingers were clinging to his shirt. And she was weeping.

"It's all right, Julia," he murmured, pressing his face close to hers. "Everything's all right."

"It's not all right!" she answered, with surprising tartness, despite her tears, and the fact that her teeth chattered as she spoke.

And he'd never been so glad to hear a human voice in his life.

"Of course it's all right," he said.

"No!" she protested. "It's not! I was so stupid and so wrong! I should have believed you about Brayles. I'm so sorry. More sorry than I can say."

Perhaps she wasn't in shock after all.

Marcus found himself smiling. Even cold and soaked through and having spent Lord knows how long fighting for her life, she wanted to *argue* with him.

"You don't need apologies with me," he said. "Not ever. Besides, it's over now. You're safe."

She sniffled. "I was going to take him down with me, Holsworth. I remembered what you said, about me being formidable. And so I *was*."

He laughed. "You are formidable because you have always been so, Lady Grantleigh, not because I said so."

She shook her head stubbornly. He felt the friction of it against his chest, and it made his heart dance. "It gave me courage, though," she said. "It *did*. And I wasn't so afraid."

"That's my girl." He rubbed his hands more vigorously over her back, relieved to feel that her body wasn't nearly as cold as it had been at first.

Suddenly self-conscious, he glanced over at their driver.

What on earth must Edgerton be thinking there beside them, listening to all this? But either the man was still too lost in thought about his brother to notice, or he wasn't as horrified as Marcus would have thought at seeing the Countess of Grantleigh seated so comfortably on the lap of the son of a freehold farmer, bantering with him on such intimate terms.

How very strange.

But then again, Edgerton had never once tormented him in boyhood. And after Marcus took his commission in the army, Edgerton had always treated him with the same respect he gave to any other officer.

Maybe there was some hope for them after all.

"Holsworth," said Julia from beneath the cover of the coats. "How did you *find* me? I sent you away! I thought I might never see you again!"

"Oh, Julia, didn't you listen to a single word I said this morning? I told you, it was impossible for me to leave you. Impossible, while you were in danger."

"But you sent your valet to pack your things!"

"To move them to the Boar's Head, no farther. After you ran back to the Hall, I gave him those orders, then got my horse and rode for Edgerton Park. It seemed the most logical place to start looking for Brayles. And, as it turns out, Lord Edgerton believed as I did, that his brother was up to no good."

Edgerton shifted a bit uncomfortably in the driving seat. "My apologies, Lady Grantleigh, for the state of my brother's morals," he said, then lapsed back into his silence again.

"Edgerton and I rode out together towards Axminster," Marcus said, "to see if we could intercept Brayles on one of the roads from London, but soon learned he'd been spotted at an inn there two nights before. We raced back to Grantleigh, thinking he might be trying to break in to get the ledgers. And we found the whole house in an uproar. Apparently, Brayles had been *invited* in, a guest under your roof. You may imagine the distress I felt at learning that."

"It was complicated," said Julia miserably from beneath the coats.

"The rest of the household would still have been fast asleep, but they were awakened shortly before we arrived by one of Brayles' servants arguing with Brayles' sister over whether or not he'd carry her trunk out to their coach. Unfortunately, by the time Lady Lambert, Lady Eleanor and Mr. Maji made it downstairs, the Brayles family and coach and trunk and all had vanished clean away. And so, even more unfortunately, had *you*."

"I'm sorry," said Julia.

"I won't soon forget the horror of learning that news," he said. "*Good God.*"

"I'm *very* sorry. But that still doesn't explain how you *found* me," she insisted. "I thought for sure I was dead on that godforsaken road."

"Ah! Well, you have Lady Lambert to thank for that. She seemed utterly convinced by the state of your *writing desk drawer*, of all things, that you'd been taken to the dower house. And so Edgerton and I raced there as fast as our mounts would carry us. Once we arrived, it was a simple matter of tracking. The curricle left a clear trail of wheel marks in the mud. And Brayles is a distinctly terrible driver. This poor horse was clearly half out of its wits."

To his great satisfaction, Julia gave a little chuckle against his chest.

The next bit of the story might be better left unsaid, he thought, at least while Edgerton was right here beside them. Marcus himself did not particularly care to relive those endless seconds in which they crept slowly closer to Brayles, having to watch him hold Julia by her hair and force her so treacherously close to the edge of that gorge, while they waited for a decent shot at him.

In the end, it was Edgerton who had the proper angle.

And the viscount was enough of a soldier to take his shot unflinchingly, and hit his target square.

Poor man.

Would the sight of his brother falling from that ledge ever leave off haunting him?

Edgerton glanced over now, as though the exact same thoughts were running through his mind. "Lady Grantleigh" he said, in a very somber tone. "I hope someday you will be able to forgive my family. I hope some day you will be able to forgive *me*. I knew what kind of man my brother was. He had no character, even as a boy. I'd hoped sending him to India would force him to better himself, but it only brought out the worst. I should have clapped him in irons years ago. I should have turned him in to the authorities myself when your husband showed me those ledgers. But—he was my brother. And I love my two nieces more than anything in the world. I thought perhaps I could reform him. And—I waited too long."

Julia had gone very still on Marcus's lap again. "He killed Christopher," she said, her voice breaking. "He *killed* him."

Marcus found her hand with his and squeezed it tight. His own heart ached, and his throat constricted. "We heard that," he said. "We heard all that Brayles said to you."

"Forgive me," Edgerton pleaded once more. "I had no idea till tonight that George had done that, that George was *capable* of that. Grantleigh had been our friend, all our lives. And he was the very best of men."

Julia's fingers clung so hard to Marcus's, he thought she might crack them in two, and she sobbed softly into his shirt.

But her other hand slid suddenly around Marcus's waist, and she pulled herself even tighter against him.

"*One* of the best," she said quietly but surely.

And—impossible at it seemed with all the awful things that had happened tonight, and with all the weight of their shared grief—Marcus sensed a sort of blossoming in the world around them, as if a whole new universe was suddenly springing to life, bright and full of hope.

"Only *one* of the best," Julia said again, and pressed a kiss to his throat.

CHAPTER 14

*A*lthough it was still the dead of night when the curricle pulled up outside Grantleigh Hall, it was immediately clear that none of the residents had gone back to sleep.

As Marcus swung Julia up in his arms again and carried her over the threshold of the Hall, Christopher's aunts, Mr. Maji, the majority of the household servants, and quite a few members of the local militia, dressed in full uniform, crowded around her.

One particular housemaid, a sour-faced girl named Louise, was nowhere to be seen, and Julia suspected the girl would never show her face in Devon again.

Everyone clamored with questions, and she could hear Captain Lowell reporting to Lord Edgerton that Miss Brayles and the little girls and the servants who'd traveled with them had still not been found, despite several patrols being dispatched to search for them.

"Try the Seaton Bridge," Julia said, from the shelter of Marcus's arms. "She was told to wait there under the willows." But somehow she thought Miss Brayles might have disobeyed that order, too. The bridge was near enough to the river road that she might well have heard the rifle shot that killed her brother, and that may have convinced her to get herself and her nieces out of the country while she could, before the authorities relieved them of all that ill-gotten gold and silver.

By this point, Marcus was clearly growing impatient with the crowd. She could feel the growing tension in his body as he held her. "Is the hearth lit in Lady Grantleigh's chamber?" he asked Aunt Margaret.

"Oh, yes," said Margaret, patting him on the arm. "We thought we'd best keep the room warm in hopes she'd soon come safely home. And, see, Marcus, you have brought her. We knew you would, dear boy. We knew you would!"

"I will carry her up," said Marcus, his deep voice carrying over the cacophony of the crowd. "Lady Margaret, Lady Eleanor, if you will, please follow us so you can tend to her."

Oh, thought Julia. *He wishes for the Aunts to tend me? Does he plan to leave me again?*

She didn't want him to let go of her.

But once the group of them had reached the upstairs hallway outside her room—Mr. Maji trailing behind his wife to join them, too—Marcus turned back to the trio of gray-haired folk. "Thank you," he said, "for providing an appearance of respectability in front of all those witnesses downstairs. But I'll ask all three of you to please return immediately to your own beds. I shall take good care of Lady Grantleigh now, I promise."

A hot blush spread over Julia's face. Anyone with half a brain knew what sort of *care* a virile man was likely to offer a lonely widow in the privacy of her bedchamber.

But none of the three older people so much as batted an eyelash.

"Excellent thinking," said Lady Eleanor, grinning. She

took hold of Mr. Maji's hand and cheerfully led him off down the hall.

Margaret stayed beside them a moment longer, blushing a bit. She leaned in close to Marcus's ear and whispered. "I'm all for it, lad. But you must promise me you'll speak with the parson first thing tomorrow morning. This is not a house given to debauchery."

Julia couldn't help herself—she laughed. "Oh, you have no idea, Aunt. You have no idea at all."

Margaret's jaw dropped, and she clapped a hand over her gaping mouth, but thankfully there was twinkling amusement in her eyes.

"I'll make her an honest woman," Marcus promised, "if she'll let me."

And not pausing even to say goodnight, he carried her over the threshold of her room, pushed the door shut definitively behind them, and they were quite alone.

And—at least at first—it seemed he really did mean that he was going to take care of her, just as the Aunts would have done. He stripped a blanket from the bed and carried her before the fire, ordering her to stand as close to the flames as she could tolerate.

"Get out of those wet clothes," he commanded, tugging loose the sash of her robe himself and stripping it from her shoulders. Before she could so much as reach for the hem of her nightdress, he seized that too in both fists, and made short work of pulling it up and over her head.

For one quick moment, she was quite naked before his gaze, and suddenly she didn't feel chilled in the slightest. But he was diligent in trying to warm her, and draped the big heavy blanket over her shoulders, pulling it closed over her front.

And then he put his arms around her again, around her and the blanket both, and bear-hugged her as though the force of that alone could squeeze the heat and life back into her.

She laughed to herself. She truly did appreciate the consideration he was showing her, but after all the events of the last day and night, what she most desperately needed from him right now was something else entirely.

"Your clothes are wet, too," she told him impishly, reaching out from under the blanket to run a hand down his damp back, and over the breeches that clung tightly to his buttocks. "I think you really must take them off."

He looked down at himself, his expression genuinely surprised. Apparently, it hadn't occurred to him that he also had been out in the wet and the cold and the wind. Or that he'd been riding hell for leather on horseback, charging through the dark on that dangerous ridge.

"Get them off," she said again. "I can help you with the boots, if you like. I'm actually quite talented at that."

The look he gave her was blazing hot. "Are you?" he said.

"I'll show you," she said. "But shirt off first."

He smiled, and it was the sort of smile that made her toes curl. "You're sure you won't be mortified by the sight of my bare chest?"

She bit at her lip. "I'll try to contain my maidenly blushes."

And with an inhaled roar of breath, he seized his own hem and all but tore his shirt off over his head. And, oh, he really was unbelievably beautiful. His huge broad shoulders and the sculpted plains of his chest and stomach glowed like bronze in the firelight.

"Goodness," she said, "I feel much better already."

"So do I," he said.

Oh, Lord. She wanted to throw her arms around him right this moment and pull him down into a kiss. But she had to go about this properly. He was going to be well and truly naked this time, every inch of him.

"Now sit in that chair." She planted a palm on his chest as she had that night in the hothouse room, and shoved him backwards onto the seat. "I'll need to get your boots off."

"How do you propose to do that, my lady, wrapped in a blanket as you are?" He leaned back, watching her lazily, his eyes hooded. But she saw the fire kindling in their dark depths.

"Let's see how I manage," she said. And keeping the blanket closed around her with her left hand, she made a show of pulling at the first boot he proffered, using only her right.

The boot didn't budge, of course.

"That's not working so well," he teased. "You might need the second hand."

"As you wish, sir," she answered. She leaned down over the boot again, this time grasping the heel in one palm and the bit behind his calf with the other, and giving just the perfect combination of pull and twist she'd learned to use with Christopher, on those nights when he preferred to dismiss his valet early and spend more time alone with her.

The boot slipped off quite neatly.

As did her blanket.

Marcus made a growling noise in his throat as his gaze trailed its way slowly down her naked body. The color had come up in his cheeks, and his breathing had gone rather rough, and it was very clear this time he had no intention of urging her to put the blanket back on.

"Your other boot, sir?" she said insouciantly, and turned around this time, displaying her backside as she repeated her trick of twist and pull.

That boot, too, slipped free.

"Damn it all," he swore.

When she turned back around again, the front panel of Marcus's breeches was quite remarkably transformed—the fall was stretched almost to bursting with the enormous evidence of his arousal.

Her heartbeat stuttered and her throat went dry. Last time, she had *felt* him as he entered her, but she hadn't had a chance to *see* him. The idea of having him displayed before her in his full masculine glory frightened her a little, and roused her almost beyond belief.

"I believe it is time for you to get out of those wet breeches, sir."

She didn't have to ask twice. He rose from the chair with confident swagger, and began to undo the buttons of his fall. *Hell and blazes*, how far they'd come from just last night, when watching him undo the buttons of his uniform coat had nearly sent her into an apoplexy.

She still trembled now as she watched him, but it was a very different sort of trembling.

Oh, how she wanted him inside her again.

One button more, and his manhood sprang free. And he was indeed magnificent, all of him, his breadth, and his muscle, and his glowing flesh, and his huge, heavy arousal jutting forward as though it, too, longed for them to be joined again.

He stripped his breeches and stockings quickly down his legs and kicked them away, stepping forward naked as the first man in the garden. And then she didn't know which of them moved first—they seemed to be in each other's arms before either had time to move, and their flesh pressed together along the full length of their bodies.

Her arms were around his neck, and his mouth was on hers, his hands roaming down her back to fit themselves possessively around her buttocks. Gripping her with his two huge palms, he lifted her upwards, and for a moment, she thought he might just do as she'd fantasized for that brief moment when they were alone at the folly—urge her to wrap her legs around his waist and plunge inside her, standing just as they were. His arms were certainly more than strong enough.

To her surprise, though, he set her back on her feet, and sank slowly to his own knees, trailing kisses down her throat, across her breasts, then over the curves of her waist and belly.

"I didn't get to see this part of you before," he murmured, rocking back on his heels for a moment to gaze at her. His eyes followed as his fingers skimmed up and down the line of her waist and across to her navel, his feather-light touch sending waves of sensation coursing through her, making her nipples tighten, and the place between her thighs grow hot and wet.

And then his mouth went lower, as his hands parted her legs.

And, *oh*.

His tongue was on her again, and she wasn't sure she could take this standing up.

If his fingers on her waist had created strong sensation, this hot, slick stroking was of another magnitude of intensity. Her eyes slid shut and her mouth fell open on a gasp, and renewed heat poured through her, making her begin to dissolve and melt as though she were made of sugar candy.

How was he doing what he was doing, licking and sucking and kissing at her all at once? Even with her eyes tight closed, the world went scarlet, glowing brilliantly as embers, and all the melting heat inside her made her flesh seem fluid, pulses and waves of it surging through her so her breasts seemed to swell, her cheeks flushed, her hands and feet tingled. And then, suddenly, all of it drew downward, inward, pulling toward that place where his mouth was, immensely heavy and weightless at the same time.

Her fingers gripped tight to the thickness of his hair as his mouth drove her to the brink of madness caress by caress.

And she must have been closer to the brink than she thought, because before she was quite aware it was coming, the pleasure burst through her body in an overwhelming rush, as though the force of it had been building up forever behind a wall which buckled and came crashing down in the space of a moment. She spasmed against him, crying out. And if he hadn't clutched her hips to hold her upright, she would have fallen straight through the floor. Straight through the crust of the earth, maybe.

His mouth stayed on her, but more gently now, his tongue stroking more lightly as smaller shocks pulsed through her, one after the other.

"Marcus," she said, moaning. "Sweet Marcus."

After a few moments more, his palm went where his mouth had been, its less intense pressure shepherding her though a few more deep throbs of pleasure, each of which drew a new, soft cry from her lips.

It seemed to go on and on and on.

She'd never imagined such a thing was possible.

When at last she had quieted, he kissed her tenderly on the inside of her thigh. "Not cold anymore, are you?" he asked.

"Not cold," she said, feeling too soft and languid to banter with him. "Not cold at all."

She rested her hands on his shoulders, still not quite trusting to the steadiness of her legs. And as she did so, she noticed her left wrist.

"My bracelet!" she exclaimed. "My bracelet! It's gone!"

Marcus scrambled to his feet, taking her wrist in his fingers. They could both plainly see her wrist was bare.

"What happened to it?" he asked.

"I have no idea," she said, still staring at the place where it had been, scarcely able to adjust her mind to the idea that the gleaming gold circlet wasn't there anymore. "I tried and tried so many times to take it off, and it wouldn't move. And now I didn't try, and—and it's *vanished*."

"I don't understand," said Marcus.

"Wait, though," she said, thinking back over the wild events of the night. "When Brayles was with me in the parlor, I took hold of the fireplace poker and tried to knock him down."

"You *what*?"

"It wasn't a successful effort, believe me," she said. "He grabbed me by the wrist, very roughly, and hit me on the back with his gun, and I fell onto an enormous traveling trunk that Miss Brayles had left open on the floor. My arm hit it so hard, I thought the bone might crack, and—well, I wasn't *thinking* about the bracelet. I was thinking about Brayles with his pistol against my temple, about to shoot me and—"

"I wish Edgerton hadn't killed him!" Marcus said, his mouth gone hard with fury. "Now I want to go back and kill him myself."

"No, *listen*!" she said. "I think the bracelet must have come loose then. Brayles' grabbing my wrist must have opened the mechanism somehow, and then my arm striking the edge of the trunk must have sent the bracelet flying off." Suddenly, she was laughing. "Oh, Lord! I think it fell inside! I think Miss Brayles is going to get a *very* interesting surprise when she opens that trunk again!"

"Miss *Brayles*? No!" said Marcus contemptuously. "She's not worthy of that bracelet!"

"Then someone else will find it," said Julia, still giddily amused. "Someone who *is* worthy. Imagine that—the enchanted bracelet heading off to the New World. What would Bharati think?"

"I don't know," he said, sounding somewhat more molli-fied, as he drew her naked body back into his arms. "But I think she would be pleased."

His mouth found hers again, and within moments, desire flared between them once more. He was still hard and urgent against her, not having found his own release, and she didn't resist in the slightest when he lifted and carried her to the bed, eased her down upon the mattress, and stretched out his body over hers.

His hands were everywhere then, exploring her, and she made bold with his flesh as well, touching him where she hadn't been able to before, stroking her palms along his powerful thighs, brushing them over the taut curve of his powerful buttocks.

And as fully as he'd pleasured her just moments before, she wanted him again. And she wanted to make him fall apart as completely as he'd done to her.

She eased her legs open, and his hips slid snugly between them, cradled by her thighs. His arousal pressed hard and hot against her belly, and he thrust against her, groaning, still kissing her, his tongue plundering her mouth.

Lord, she wanted him inside her, *now*, quickly.

But, as always, he seemed to have his own plan in mind. He rolled sideways on the bed, pulling her with him, until he was the one with his back on the mattress, and she was above him, her legs straddling his.

He looked up at her with eyes full of desire, but also of question, and for the first time since their clothing had come off, he went very still.

"I'm sorry you lost your bracelet," he said quietly.

Julia nestled down against him, her breasts against his chest, and pressed kisses to his throat. "I don't think I need it anymore. I think it's done its work for us." She shifted her hips, bringing the part of her still wet from the ministrations of his mouth against the jutting hardness of his shaft. She rocked against him, letting her slick flesh slide up and down the hot length of him without him actually entering her.

He groaned again, his arms shaking. But, much as it was clear he wanted to, he didn't act on the invitation she was offering.

Instead, he took hold of her wrists, urging her to be still, urging her upright.

"Look at me, Julia," he said, his eyes intent on hers. "I want you to be *sure*. Before we go any farther, even tonight."

"Sure of what?"

"Sure you want me. *Me*, as I am. You know I love you, Julia. I've told you and I've showed you in every way I know how, and I'd happily spend the rest of my life finding infinitely many more ways to show you. But I'm not Christopher. And I can't be Christopher. I'm not asking you to stop loving him, because I don't think that a love like that ever dies. I'm just asking you to—"

"Love you, too? Oh, Marcus, I—"

He cut her off. "Don't speak too quickly, please. I want you to *think*. Chris was—an *easier* man than I am. Life with me would be difficult in many ways, and I don't only mean because of the way Society might treat us. I mean because I am—"

"More tempestuous?" she said. "More intense?"

"Yes, both of those things."

"More passionate, perhaps?" she said, trailing her fingers over the remarkable contours of his chest. "More demanding?" And she raised up on her knees a bit so that she could slip her hand between them and grasp the thickness of his shaft. "More *challenging*?"

"God, Julia," he gasped, his head arching back into the pillow. "Don't *do* that right now. I am trying very hard to be noble."

"Very hard is the right phrase for it," she teased, but he was clearly in no mood for joking.

"*Think*, Julia," he demanded. "Please."

Oh, poor Marcus. Did he really not understand what she felt? Even now?

She supposed she needed to tell him.

So she drew a deep breath and gazed down at him, laying her palms to either side of his face. "You look at me, now," she said. "And really listen. Will you?"

"Yes," he said. And his eyes were so full of uncertainty, and readiness for what she now knew was all-too-familiar pain.

"Marcus Holworth," she told him, willing him to see deep inside her, willing him to recognize the truth of her words, "you are an extraordinary man. I always understood that in the past, though you terrified me. But I saw another side of it when you comforted me when I was falling apart last night. And then tonight—well, it's remarkable how an hour or so feeling quite certain one is about to die can clarify one's thoughts. I see it all now, and I know it with all my heart. You call something out in my soul that I've never known before. I do want you, and with much more than my body. I am sure about you. And, Marcus, I *do* love you."

He let out a sigh that sounded great enough to crack his heart in two. "Do you mean that?"

"I mean that. I *love* you. I love the sheer, vital force of life in you, and the intelligence in you and the poetry and the fierceness and the loyalty in you. And I want to spend my life with you, too, finding infinite ways to show you. You're right —the love I had for Christopher can never truly die. But the world I lived in with him isn't my world anymore. There's no life for me that way. But you and I, Marcus, we can build a new world together. A world of our own."

"Oh, God," he said, squeezing shut his eyes, "I *want* that, Julia. I want that with everything in me."

"Then it's ours," she told him, and kissed him long and hard. "It will always be ours."

And then she sat upright again, and urged her hips once more against his rock-hard manhood.

"And now, for the love of heaven," she said, "tell me you're about to make mad, passionate love to me."

"Oh, I'm about to," he swore fervently.

"Thank heaven!"

"But I must share a poem with you first."

"Holsworth! I don't *need*—"

"It's not for you," he said, laughing. "It's for me. It's one of Bharati's—and it's short, I promise you. But when I first read it, all I could think of was you. And I've thought of it so many times since. You see, in the Prakrit poetry Bharati modeled her verses on—"

"Holsworth! You're not about to deliver a *lecture* to me?"

"No. I'm just telling you, in this tradition, the poet can speak in any number of voices, and this one is written in the voice of the man she loves, as he prepares to make love to her."

"Oh," said Julia, intrigued despite herself. "Well, then, go on."

Instead of reciting the promised poem, though, Holsworth speared his fingers through the still-damp tangles of her hair and combed them gently out, spreading her curls across her shoulders, and then drawing the greater mass of them forward so they spilled down across his chest.

Julia sighed, and rocked her hips against him again. "*Maddening*, Holsworth—can I add that to the list of words I used to describe you? Because if this poem is all that's standing in the way of you making love to me again, you'd better get reciting."

"I'm ready now," he said, and in that deep, gorgeous voice of his that always made her rib cage vibrate, he spoke the poem at last:

> *"Her loosened hair tumbles over my chest*
> *Like warm spring rain,*
> *Each strand a drop*
> *That makes fresh roots surge."*

"Oh," said Julia, sighing. "Is that all of it?"

"Yes," he said. "Just those four lines."

"And that made you think of me?"

"It did. Because that's what you are to me, sweetheart—life-giving and warm, like the spring rain. You make me want to live, *really* live, and you make me believe life can bring abundance."

"It does," she promised him, her heart suddenly full to overflowing. "It will."

"And as it turns out," he added, smiling up at her. "I do truly love seeing you with your hair loosened. And I adore the feel of it against my chest."

"That's good."

"Now come here," he demanded, drawing her down towards him.

"I like that poem," she whispered as she complied, and she shook her hair so it tumbled down slowly over his shoulders and his face as well, drop after drop after drop.

And he did surge then, taking hold of her hips and driving inside her at last, making her moan. And she rode him as he thrust into her again and again, in a glorious rhythm that seemed just perfectly their own, and that would bring them together in joyful madness all through the rest of their lives.

Author's Note:

If you enjoyed this book, please take a moment and leave a review on Amazon! Reviews are essential for helping new readers find my books, which makes it possible for me to devote time to writing the next one!

I deeply appreciate all reviews.